Mah Jongg Posse

Tatiana Zurkiewicz

To All my Mah Jongg playing friends from the Midwest to Pepeekeo, HI

CHAPTER 1

The Break in period

I was pleasantly surprised to receive a call asking me to join a Mah Jongg group as a substitute. Earlier in the year I watched the group play weekly at a quaint little coffee shop, near the hospital where I took my aunt for treatment. It wasn't until one of the players, Kat, approached me and started a conversation that I was asked to join the group. Once I told her that I played Mah Jongg she said that they always needed a few substitutes and asked if I would be interested. Of course, I immediately said yes.

Kat may or may not have realized that for over six months prior I had sat listening in on the Mah Jongg group's conversations while waiting for my aunt at the same time as they were playing each week. Of course, when Kat asked me if I would be interested in substituting I could not have been happier to not only play Mah Jongg but to be part of a group of women who I had come to admire from afar.

The regular group consisted of an older woman in her sixties, who they called Mrs. M., and two other younger women, besides Kat who were probably in their thirties. One of the women, Ellen was a married mom of three who worked part-time, the other two, Molly and Kat, were single career women. From my previous observations, Ellen referred to as Molly was her sister-in-law and Kat as her future sister-in-law (Kat was engaged to Ellen's brother Chuck).

Molly was actually the sister of Ellen's brother-in-law, but Ellen still considered Molly to be her sister-in-law, a term of endearment that I am sure Molly appreciated. In an interesting twist, the last I heard Mrs. M. had visited Portugal with Ellen's uncle Stan so some romance may or may not have been brewing in that area.

The first time I arrived to substitute in the Mah Jongg game I was greeted warmly by Kat, who had invited me into the group. She introduced me to the other players, Mrs. M. and Ellen, and mentioned that I was substituting for Molly. Mrs. M. sat across from me at the table and subtly peppered me with questions throughout the game. I attempted to keep my answers short as I had always been taught to keep the chatter down during the game.

"So how long have you been playing Mah Jongg, Darcy?" Mrs. M. asked me directly.

I replied, "About thirty years, but I had a few years when I couldn't play due to lack of a group to play with, so I have only been back into it for the last five years or so. I'm so happy that Northern Michigan is such a hotbed for Mah Jongg. Who would have thought? Of course, most of the people in my family play."

"Where is your family from?" asked Mrs. M.

I answered, "My mom was born in Newaygo, so mostly on the west side of the state."

"Interesting," Ellen noted. "You know that we have been playing in this group in one form or another for about twenty years."

I replied, "That is a long time."

Kat laughed, "Well I just started playing last fall with the group, but I learned to play when I was about twelve years old or so. We have another friend who was the one who taught me to play but she won't be substituting for a while. She just had twins within the last couple of months. She has her hands full."

"Yikes," I said, not letting on that I knew anything about that whole three sets of twins' drama which had played itself out when I was observing the group.

Ellen laughed, "That is our friend, Alexis, she has three sets of twins. The first set is done with college, the second set is in high school and then she has the new babies, Josey and Jake, they are very cute, those two. It is quite a thing."

"Don't forget Lisa," added Ellen. She turned to me and remarked "Lisa is Mrs. M.'s daughter-in-law and she substitutes in the group sometimes too. Now Lisa is an excellent player, much like Molly who you are substituting for now. Molly has a busy schedule so she can't always get away."

"Understood," I noted.

Mrs. M. asked, "So is your schedule pretty flexible?"

I answered, "I teach online and occasionally I teach a class on campus so there are days when I'm just swamped with work and other days when I have lots of time. It really depends upon how many classes I

3

have and at what point in the semester we happen to be in. Please feel free to call or text me anytime. If I'm free, I will be here."

Mrs. M. replied, "That's good to know. In all the time we have been playing, we have had a few new players, but mostly the circle is small. The fact that you know how to play is a bonus. Honestly, teaching someone to play is just exhausting. Do you ladies remember my friend Stella? She wanted to learn to play and then once she came to the group, she stated it was just too hard to learn. I mean the woman has a master's degree in business or something, you would think that she could have been able to handle a little Mah Jongg. She never returned after we taught her and then I just stopped asking. I guess you can only do what you can do with some people."

Kat nodded, "That being said, you know Ellen is our most reliable player. She rarely misses a game. Now, some people just go flitting off to Portugal at the drop of a hat, so it is good that we have a few substitutes just in case."

"I'm not saying that won't happen again," Mrs. M. noted. "Portugal was fun and now I'm thinking about Spain. I don't think that I must keep everyone apprised of my schedule, if I'm gone, I'm gone, enough said."

The other ladies laughed. Kat leaned in towards me and explained, "Mrs. M. has become a world traveler, and we're obligated to give her a hard time about it due to the fact that she just took off earlier this year with Ellen's uncle Stan for a trip. No advanced notice

to the Mah Jongg women, she just skipped the country."

"Guilty," replied Mrs. M.

CHAPTER 2

An Earthly Creature

I was delighted that I was called upon the very next week to substitute for Molly again. Little was mentioned about her absence, and I did not let on that I knew anything about her. What I did know was that she had been in treatment for a second bout with breast cancer despite her young age. I wondered if her health was improving since she had been quite ill.

Molly had missed many games of Mah Jongg as a result of her diagnosis earlier in the year, but it seemed that she was getting better the last time I saw her from afar while observing the group several months before. Still, with no new information from the other players I was unsure.

Once again Mrs. M. sat across from me and subtly interrogated me throughout the game. Ellen actually got the ball rolling by asking me if I was married. I told her that I was and asked if she was. She replied yes and mentioned that Kat was currently engaged and that made Kat blush.

I asked Kat "How long have you been engaged?"

"Three months," Kat noted. "I was actually engaged right here in this very spot," she noted pointing to the chair where she was sitting. "It is as Ellen says, a very sappy story."

I told her, "I would love to hear it someday." While the words are coming out of my mouth, I'm thinking of my sister telling me that when I play with this group for at least the first few times to not talk too much and not win too much. At that point, the conversation moved on.

"The most exciting part of the whole thing is that Kat is going to be joining our family soon. I'm sure that I have mentioned that Molly is my sister-in-law so now I will have two Mah Jongg playing sisters-in-law. In terms of the engagement of Chuck and Kat itself, I for one did not see that coming." sighed Ellen.

I asked, "Why not?"

"Ellen had to eat her words on that one," Mrs. M. explained with a smile. "She was so sure that her brother Chuck would never settle down and then poof, he and Kat were engaged."

Ellen told us, "In my defense, how was I to know that Chuck would turn from a dog-borrowing playboy to a sensible, love-struck guy in a short six months or so? Honestly, who knew?"

"He wasn't so much a playboy. There was just that awful fiancé, of his, Aurora." Mrs. M. commented.

Kat piped up, "I wouldn't say too much bad about her. I mean he loved her at one time, and it just was not a good match. I give her the benefit of the doubt, but I hope to God I never run into her."

"If that does happen," noted Mrs. M. "I'm one hundred percent sure that you could take her. She is tall but spindly. You on the other hand are scrappy. I don't think that she has it in her to mount a defense. Of

7

course, if she does have any fight in her and you will need backup, you know that Ellen and I are always here for you."

Ellen smiled, "The Mah Jongg Posse is strong and ready to help out at any time."

Kat laughed, "I doubt it will come to blows, even if I run into her. For one thing, she is the one who broke the engagement. Also, let's not forget, she doesn't even know me. She thought that Chuck was dating Molly. Maybe we should alert Molly to be on the lookout for Aurora, especially in the greater Grand Rapids area."

"You would not believe this woman," added Ellen directing her comments to me. "She came barging in here a few months back, now keep in mind she and my brother had broken up more than a year earlier, and her attitude was just rude. She made a big dramatic presentation of dropping the engagement ring Chuck gave her onto Molly's Mah Jongg card."

Kat lifted her hand to show me the ring and added, "I have always wondered about that. Why did she think that Chuck was dating Molly?"

"She is an airhead, that's why," replied Ellen. She then turned to me, unaware of course, that I had seen the whole thing go down because I was there that day waiting for my aunt. "My brother's ex-fiancee apparently could not believe that an earthly creature like Kat could steal my brother's heart. That woman was a menace. You know she never did want to learn to play Mah Jongg."

I noted, "That tells you all you ever need to know

about her."

Everyone laughed, including Mrs. M., who gave me a silent nod of approval.

CHAPTER 3

Jury Duty Curse

The weather was rainy, and I walked into the coffee shop a little wet from it. I know I looked soggy, even by Northern Michigan standards. The other ladies were already there and had the game set up. They greeted me politely and Kat mentioned that there were excellent brownie samples at the front counter.

Everyone laughed. Although a petite woman, Kat was a big fan of all baked goods, and since samples were always available at the front of the bakery, she had a running commentary concerning their taste and texture.

Mrs. M. once again sat across from me and waited just long enough to not seem pushy to ask me about my family. I explained that my sister was a judge, and my husband was a lawyer. "So, you didn't pursue the law?" asked Mrs. M.

I laughed, "Honestly, I don't even like to be called for jury duty. These days they take one look at my name and excuse me right off the jump. You know my husband loves the law and so does my sister but for me the law seems just so dense and boring to keep my attention for very long."

"Oh my gosh," noted Ellen. "Do you guys remember when I was called to jury duty several years ago?"

Mrs. M. replied "I do remember that. You were so sure that you were going to get out of it, and you ended up on a four-week trial. How did that ever come out? I don't remember."

"All I can say is that I learned to knit from that one lady on our panel, as for the rest of it was just a boring blur," Ellen replied. "The funny part was that on our last day of deliberations we were sitting up in the court building and coincidentally the circus came to town that day and they were setting up in the street below. All I could think of was this is a strange juxtaposition. The trial was sort of a circus and now the actual circus was here in town."

Mrs. M. questioned, "I'm trying to remember what happened after that."

"We found the guy guilty, and I went back to work," Ellen responded. "Then again, through no fault of my own and coincidentally, three of my coworkers were called to jury duty the very next month. They teased me for many months about how I infected them with the jury duty curse. It was quite a thing; I never lived it down and it wasn't even my fault."

Kat laughed, "I bet your bosses loved that, all those people being gone at the same time."

"Two of the three were excused for various reasons," Ellen replied. "Only one person was placed on a panel and had to serve for several weeks. On the positive side, she met a guy there and ended up dating. So much for the jury duty curse."

Mrs. M. noted, "I think that whole building you were in was cursed. Remember how someone firebombed the Parole Office that your agency shared a wall with? Talk about having like 400 suspects. Did they ever get to the bottom of that?"

"There were lots of unintended consequences," Ellen replied. "First of all, the arson squad found so many violations on our side of the wall when they were investigating that they actually walked us through the building pointing things out. People had space heaters under their desks, small fridges that were giving off heat in small spaces and the like. The worst thing was the guy who sat a few cubicles down from me."

Kat asked, "What was that about? I vaguely remember that."

"In almost any building they have built in battery powered security lights. They look like the rest of the overhead lights, but they stay on in an emergency or outage," explained Ellen. "The guy who sat a few cubicles down from me had a safety light above his desk. He thought that the lighting was 'too harsh' for his sensitive eyes, and due to his boo-hoo attitude he took the actual fluorescent bulbs out of the light fixture above his desk without permission. You should have seen these big burley arson guys dressing him down about taking the bulbs out. I remember that they told him very specifically that they would be making 'spot checks' in the future. They never did come back as far as I know, and the agency moved out of that building."

Kat remarked, "And the arson?"

"Unsolved," replied Ellen. "Maybe that building

was cursed. However, the new building has those desks that you can see everyone's legs underneath, perhaps a result of the whole space heater debacle in the old building. I still do a little part-time work over there and it is a whole different modern vibe. I would love to turn off the lights and see if that guy took the bulbs out again."

Mrs. M. mused, "You don't quit, do you?"

"Safety first," Ellen responded.

CHAPTER 4

The Secret Crush

I was surprised that the ladies contacted me for the fourth week in a row to substitute for Mah Jongg and I wondered to myself how Molly was doing since they did not mention her. I had two schools of thought, either she was ill again, and I did not know these women well enough to be let in on that information or she was just busy with her job.

It was a typical Michigan summer, always there was lots of traffic and tourists, especially on the weekends. Friday and Monday traffic was even heavier in our little rural area because people were rushing up to Traverse City or Charlevoix.

I arrived at the coffee shop a little early and sat down with an iced tea to take it in for a moment. It was one of the oldest buildings in town from what I had been told and may have originally been a soda fountain/drug store. It had the original floors, and they creaked a little sometimes depending upon the weather. The door had not been replaced from the original building, and it also creaked a little at times. They had replaced the old soda fountain area with large glass cases that showcased their bakery items and there was also a nice counter.

The Mah Jongg players usually sat at one of several square tables which were nicely spaced in the front of the shop. The best feature in my opinion of the entire place was the large windows in the front which looked out on the main street of town. As I sat contemplating the past and present of the building the ladies arrived to play.

As usual, I tried to stay neatly in the background. I did a lot of smiling and nodding and despite my best efforts did not win many games. My sister would be very proud.

The big topic of the day seemed to be Ellen's children going to Zoo Camp. The kids were staying in the city with her husband's brother who was taking them to and from camp every day and sending her lots of photos. She showed one where the boys were carrying her daughter, one by her legs and one by her head out of Zoo Camp. Ellen quipped, "They know that sort of stunt would not be tolerated by me but of course their Uncle Bill doesn't have kids and doesn't know any better. I bet they are eating fast food at every meal and having ice cream right before bed every night."

Mrs. M. added, "I bet you and your husband are eating fast food every day the kids are gone and having ice cream every night before bed."

"You are half right on that one, let's just say that a nightcap before bed, when you know no one will be calling for mom is a great idea," Ellen added. "Perhaps a few nightcaps."

Mrs. M. said, "Not to change the topic but what did you ever decide on your parents' anniversary? That is coming up pretty quick."

"Kat can tell you how that is going since my brother Chuck hijacked our plans," asked Ellen. "Kat, do you have something to add?"

Kat laughed, "Do not blame me. I think that Chuck is just looking for a reason for us to go on vacation together and so he concocted this whole thing with your folks' inadvertently hijacking your plans. I was under the impression that it will be their fortieth anniversary, is that correct?"

"Yes," said Ellen. "For some reason I had it in my head that it was fifty but is just forty, it makes sense to me now."

Kat added, "Speaking of Chuck, he indicated that he would pay for everyone if you guys want to go with us. I have never been to Bermuda, so I'm stoked. Have you ever been to Bermuda, Darcy?"

I replied, "As a matter of fact I have. It is cool, just a big old rock in the middle of the ocean and for some reason, very British. I guess it was or is a possession of Britain. I can tell you two things I remember most are Cave Tours and Rum Cake."

"I can see why Kat wants to go there, if they have cake, she is always in," remarked Ellen. "How are the beaches?"

I answered, "Sadly, overall, not as good as Kauai but still nice. They have pink sand beaches, which Kauai does not have. The last time I was in Bermuda with my sister I didn't go on the helicopter ride, but they do have them, and they are supposed to be really fun. There is quite a bit to see from the air from what I understand."

"What else?" asked Kat.

I replied, "There are a few historical places, since that is my thing, I was all over that. My sister went with me and by the fourth or fifth monument, she wanted to be back at the beach or shopping district. They have old churches, the dockyard and other historical places but again, that part of it is not for everyone."

"My parents will most likely just want to be at the beach and eat out" noted Ellen. "They could do the same thing in Florida, and they wouldn't even need a passport. Of course, there is something exotic about using your passport and coming home with all sorts of fun things you purchased. Kat, I can see you coming home with a suitcase full of rum cakes and a commemorative plate with King Charles's face on it."

Kat chimed in, "King Charles, that came out of nowhere. What is up with that?"

"Now we know the truth, Ellen," Mrs. M. observed seizing on the opportunity to do a little teasing. "You have a crush on King Charles, and you want a plate with his face on it."

"Why would you think that?" asked Ellen.

Mrs. M. shot back, "Of all the things that someone could bring back from Bermuda you zero in on a plate with King Charles's face on it.I think that is sort of telling."

"Your face just lit up when we started talking about him," Kat added. "It seems you have a little crush."

Ellen said exasperated, "I do not, this is how rumors get started you know."

"You are getting quite worked up for something that is nothing," Kat said chuckling softly. "You are allowed to have a crush or two in your life."

Mrs. M. noted, "I personally am crushproof, much like those cigarette boxes."

"I personally think that you should come with a warning from the Surgeon General," noted Ellen. "Watch out, this woman is a tease."

Kat leaned over to Ellen and whispered, "I will get you a King Charles souvenir and it will be our little secret."

CHAPTER 5

Zoo Camp

It was an oppressively hot day and the air conditioning at the coffee shop was having trouble keeping up. I arrived early and sat down with an iced tea and sample chocolate cookie. When everyone arrived, I realized that once again, I was substituting for Molly. It remained a mystery where she was or why she needed a substitute.I knew enough not to ask being new to the group.

Kat asked Ellen how Zoo Camp had been for her children. Ellen laughed and remarked that the entire ride back from the city her kids were talking over each other trying to recount their adventures. There was also lots of talk about Uncle Bill. She noted "They went on and on about the lunches they provided at Zoo Camp, of all things. I'm glad that the camp provided lunch because if it was up to Uncle Bill it would have been one of those paper lunch bags with a twenty-dollar bill and a business card situation."

"Confirmed bachelor?" I inquired.

Ellen answered, "He actually lost his wife when they were newly married. It was a few years ago. That's another part of the whole story. Bill told us that the first day when he went to pick them up this female zookeeper was very friendly with him. I guess on the second day she mentioned that she was conducting a survey and wanted to know why he chose the camps he chose for his children. When he told her that they were not his children she gave it the full court press."

"Young women these days," commented Mrs. M. as she let out an exaggerated sigh.

Ellen continued, "I'm not sure what transpired overall but the kids came home with zoo hats and tote bags which I didn't pay for, and Bill was wearing a zoo hat too. According to the kids, Miss Melinda was very attentive."

"Besides teaching your boys how to pick up women, what was camp actually like?" asked Mrs. M.

Ellen replied, "Pretty good from what I could gather, of course, the boys both want to be either Zookeepers or Vets after going to those workshops. In my mind, I'm adding up the cost of Veterinary School and wondering what kind of a degree a Zookeeper would get. They grow up fast."

"What about your daughter?" asked Mrs. M.

"My little girl was enthralled by a session called Tropical Friends," Ellen explained. "She is ready to leave for the tropics today. She wants to get a parrot. She keeps bringing up fun facts about the rainforest. Kat, you may have a travel buddy for Hawaii in the future, of course she is only in elementary school, so it won't be anytime soon."

"On another topic, we are still ironing out our vacation to the sub-tropical island of Bermuda, so I'm focused on that now," declared Kat. "I'm a pretty good planner, but I really don't know your parents well enough to know what they would like, Chuck isn't sure either. We don't want to turn into one of those car breakdowns, food poisoning situations like they had on their honeymoon.I think that they were scarred for life over that. It seems like they never take vacations, at least that is what Chuck told me."

Ellen answered, "That is so true. When we were little, it was always the standard trips with the five of us all piled into the station wagon. We went camping and up north to places like Pictured Rocks and Tahquamenon Falls. Sometimes we would drive to family events, weddings and the like but I can't remember my parents going on a vacation alone. I mean we have all been out of the house for ages and they basically have time to go wherever they want whenever they want, and they don't. That being said, they seem all in for Bermuda."

"I did have one idea I wanted to run by you," Kat stated. "What are your thoughts about a fishing charter for your folks while we're in Bermuda? Do you know if either your parents or Chuck get seasick? I know your dad and Chuck fish on Lake Mitchell and Lake Cadillac in a small boat, but the ocean is a different thing. I did hear that they will grill up the fish you catch."

Ellen asked, "What if you don't catch any fish?"

"Rum cake," explained Kat

Ellen laughed, "You know you don't have to plan every moment of every day for your in-laws; they are probably able to amuse themselves."

"Doing what?" asked Kat.

Mrs. M. replied, "Duh, you know what. For pity's sake they are not elderly, they are practically my age!"

"Oh," Kat whispered blushing.

CHAPTER 6

Bermuda of the Great Lakes

The summer was winding down and everyone was trying to get all their outdoor fun in while they could. It was still a very nice day for Northern Michigan; it was in the seventies with a warm breeze. We had had several consecutive days of sunshine with rainy nights. I was enjoying my summer of playing Mah Jongg with the ladies. I was always observant of their interactions with me and with each other. They seemed to have accepted me on some level, and I enjoyed listening to all of their stories. It was becoming a highlight of my week on the weeks that I was lucky enough to play.

Having just returned from Beaver Island Ellen appeared to have a bit of a sun/wind burn. Kat had a lot of color in her face and even Mrs. M. was sporting a bit of a tan. I was the last one to arrive and I must admit the palest. We started to play and about halfway into the first game, Molly came in the door of the shop.

She was dressed for work and looked healthy. She was wearing a tailored suit in a very soft purple hue with a white shirt and white flats. Her hair had grown out some from the cancer treatments and was quite a bit longer than it had been the last time I saw her. She too was unaware as far as I knew that I had observed her playing Mah Jongg for several months prior.

Molly approached the table and stated, "I just had to stop by, I'm back on the road this afternoon for work. It has been a hectic summer that is for sure." She then turned to me and remarked, "You must be Darcy, who was described to me as a good player but *not too good*."

I laughed and answered yes. Mrs. M. then asked Molly where she was going and Molly replied "Houston, which is fine since this is all part of my new responsibilities since my promotion. I feel a little better because you have good substitutes, but I miss you guys and all your stories. I hear someone is going to Bermuda soon."

"That would be me," replied Kat. "We invited your brother and your sister-in-law Rachel, but they didn't want to go."

Molly laughed and noted, "Rachel is a little bit of a stay at home, I need to control my environment type of person. I know she does have a passport, but I doubt she has ever used it."Molly then asked Ellen, "What about you and your husband, Dean, don't you two want to go to Bermuda?"

"We just got back from Beaver Island," explained Ellen. "It is basically the same thing." To that everyone, including me, laughed.

"I guess Beaver Island is known as the Bermuda of the Great Lakes is what you are saying?" asked Molly.

Ellen replied, "Very funny. I know Darcy would like it; you constantly run into historical markers and the like. It is sort of like an island inside of a museum. There were a few sketchy lighthouses there with long windy staircases and this one really creepy house. The ferry ride was good though."

"How long is that ride?" asked Molly.

Ellen replied, "It is a couple of hours, but really fun. The kids were just so stoked to see the waves crashing over the boat and they got very excited when they started to see shore. I could not believe what a daredevil my little girl is, I can understand the boys being risk-takers, but Annie is something else."

"What did they like the best?" asked Kat.

Ellen answered, "We walked along the shoreline and took some hikes in the woods. I think that the biggest thrill was all the rocks. The kids all picked up so many rocks, every place we went they were stuffing their pockets with rocks. I had to put my foot down and tell them that they could only take 5 home each."

"That was probably a good idea," noted Mrs. M. "What are they going to do with rocks anyway, you have plenty of rocks at home."

"Well that is a very good question," Ellen noted. "Annie tried to secretly stuff her pockets with extra rocks. So, when Dean picked her up to swing her around right before we boarded the ferry, they came flying out of her pockets like a rock rocket."

"I can't imagine where she gets that outlaw behavior from," observed Mrs. M. winking at Molly.

Molly laughed, "You forget, I have a direct pipeline to your sister Rachel, and she is not afraid to spill the tea about the shenanigans that occurred when you guys were growing up. I mean besides the rowboat incident, which your parents still don't know about, there are plenty more sketchy things that happened."

"Rachel is a very unreliable source," remarked Ellen.

"Really," responded Molly. "She described the rowboat incident exactly as you did. Also, there was something about decapitating the neighbor girl's dolls."

Ellen said, "I have no idea where those doll heads are buried."

Molly shook her head knowingly and left the coffee shop.

CHAPTER 7

Keep It Clean Ladies

I hadn't played with the group for a few weeks; I thought that Molly was back or that Lisa was substituting instead. It was late September and was starting to get cool in the mornings and evenings. I had been on a short vacation to see my mother-in-law in Sarasota and was happy to get back to Michigan and my normal routine. I was anxious to play with the group and catch up with their lives.

Ellen was already at the table when I arrived, and she greeted me and asked how I had been. We exchanged pleasantries and just then Mrs. M. and her daughter-in-law arrived. Introductions were made and we settled in to play Mah Jongg.

I had seen the daughter-in-law, Lisa, when I observed the group earlier in the year. She was a very nice person but seemed to be a little fragile and slightly uncomfortable around her mother-in-law. From what I had learned in the past she was the wife of Mrs. M.'s older son although she was only in her late 20s.

Lisa had two daughters who Mrs. M. and Lisa's mother, Grandma Kay both doted on. Grandma Kay was in a book club with Ellen and had a cat named Ralph. It did not appear that Grandma Kay played

Mah Jongg although, apparently, Mrs. M. had taught Lisa to play several years prior.

Ellen explained that Kat was in Bermuda and would be for another week. Mrs. M. remarked to Ellen "I bet you are anxious for her to get back so you can get your commemorative King Charles plate."

"Very funny," retorted Ellen. "I wonder how many rum cakes she will bring back with her."

I added, "When I came back from Bermuda they had searched my luggage, I'm assuming the rum cakes were so dense that they set off some sort of alarm. There was a little note in there indicating that they had been through everything. You think that they would realize that people coming home from Bermuda would have luggage laden with heavy, dense rum cake."

"No doubt. So, Darcy, has anything exciting happened in your world since we last saw you? It has been a minute and if your life is anything like mine, it's 24/7 excitement." Ellen remarked.

I answered, "Well, my hubs and I went down to see his mom in Sarasota. Nothing to report on that trip. I sometimes feel like I'm in an alternative universe when we're down there. I think it has to do with visiting often, I have gotten used to it."

Ellen responded, "Yes, I know that feeling, familiar but not quite right. What else is going on with you?"

"Since you asked, I did have one day last week that I was hit on twice in one day," I noted as I held up my hand to show my wedding ring. I added, "It was so strange, twice in one day. Is a wedding ring not a deterrent these days?"

"Hardly," noted Lisa. "I think it encourages them sometimes. I was at the eye doctor, and he was flirting with me a little bit. I wondered why until I went out through the waiting room, and I could see that I was the only person under age 70 in there. He was probably glad to have someone who he didn't have to shout at for them to hear him."

Ellen laughed, "That is true. Of course, there are some days when you just have the kavorka. That has happened to me, I'm just minding my own business in the produce section of the Meijer store, and some guy sidles up to me and starts to chat about the size of the bananas. That sort of conversation can mean only one thing. I'm not going to abandon my cart and run away but I will get out of there ASAP. I don't have time for such foolishness."

Lisa laughed, "I guess we are all pretty irresistible at times."

"Don't laugh," stated Ellen. "I can't even wear perfume to bed on a weeknight, that is just asking for trouble if you know what I mean and I have been married a long time."

Mrs. M. interjected, "Before you add to the group chat here Lisa, keep in mind that the mother of your husband is sitting right here."

"I wouldn't think of saying a thing Mrs. M., as you know we have twin beds," mused Lisa.

Mrs. M. observed, "That explains why I only have two grandchildren."

"You two and your loose talk," remarked Ellen.

"Let's not forget we have company here; we really shouldn't be telling tales out of school with Darcy around."

Mrs. M. responded, "She is fine as far as I'm concerned." She then turned to me, waved her hand like a wand and stated, "Consider yourself officially part of the Mah Jongg Posse."

CHAPTER 8

What Kind of Cookies was That?
A Tough One.

A few weeks went by before I was asked to substitute for Mah Jongg and the weather was noticeably colder but just about right for Northern Michigan in October. I arrived at the coffee shop early and bought tea, picked up a sample of something that I thought was going to be good but as it turned out it had squash filling. As I had heard Kat say in the past, it was inspired but stupid.

Kat came in minutes after I did, she picked up a sample and walked back to the table. She explained that she had recently returned from her trip to Bermuda, and it was quite a shock to come back to the cold. Before I could ask her about her trip, Ellen and Mrs. M. came in and sat down.

As we set up the game, Mrs. M. asked Kat if she knew what was going on with Molly and the firefighter who she had been dating over the summer. Mrs. M. turned towards me and explained, "Molly bought a firefighter at the bachelor auction in the spring, they were dating but that is the last I heard about it."

Kat noted, "Molly isn't seeing him anymore. From what I could piece together, there were mother issues with him. This sounds so mean, but it sounds like his mother was concerned that Molly would not be able to deliver in the grandchildren area due to her cancer treatment. She didn't want him to get too serious with her."

"I hate that woman," remarked Ellen. "I don't even know who she is, but I really hate her."

Mrs. M. added, "These are people in their thirties, a mother should not have that much influence as far as I'm concerned. I'm speaking here from the mother of two grown boys, and I would never do something to block either one of them from getting serious with someone."

"How did Molly take the breakup?" asked Ellen.

Kat replied, "It is so hard to tell with her, I know she liked him, but she has been so focused on the cancer and on her career over the past year. They didn't even date that long. I think she valued the distraction but wasn't ready to get serious with anyone. That is aside from the mother problems which I'm sure she just let roll off her back."

"She is a tough cookie, that Molly," stated Ellen.

Kat added, "Speaking of cookies, how was that rum cake I brought from Bermuda for you?"

Ellen answered, "Of course any mention of baked goods will get a response from Kat. The rum cake was fab, you know my mom has already ordered some sort of special pans to bake rum cakes in and of course try to repeat and perfect the recipe. She went on and on about all the fun they had in Bermuda."

"It was great," noted Kat. "Your mom and I just laughed and laughed on the boat when Chuck and his dad were reeling in these large fish." Kat turned to me and explained, "Chuck is my fiancé and Ellen's brother. I'm not sure that you know that."

I remarked, "I think that was brought to my attention.I think it is nice. I love the whole sister-in-law dynamic. I have a sister-in-law I will tell you about sometime."

"Does your sister-in-law have a secret crush on King Charles that she will not fess up to?" asked Kat.

I responded, "It would not surprise me."

"Well, besides the rum cakes, which there were quite a few different varieties of, I also purchased a wonderful mug for Ellen with a King Charles picture on it in Bermuda," mentioned Kat.

Mrs. M. asked, "So just to clarify, was the picture of King Charles while he was in Bermuda or just the mug was purchased in Bermuda?"

"I doubt the photo was taken there, he was wearing a heavy robe and a crown," explained Kat. "It is one of those mugs that have a photo on the back and front, that way Ellen can look longingly at him no matter what position the mug happens to be in."

Ellen sighed, "Will I ever live this down?"

"Not as long as I'm alive," said Mrs. M.

CHAPTER 9

A Real Problem

Although it was October it was a day that was as warm and sunny as August. The leaves were changing but the weather all week had been perfect. Ellen, Kat and Mrs. M. were setting up the game when I came in. Mrs. M. explained that Molly was still out. There was some general discussion of the weather and the upcoming holiday. Before long we were chatting about Ellen's stint as a room mother for her little girl, Annie's class at school. Kat was unfamiliar with the concept.

Ellen explained, "Don't you remember from elementary school? Mostly it is moms who come to school and help the poor teacher when there is some sort of insane classroom activity which could easily turn into a riot. It is basically riot control duty and there are always snacks."

"I would sign up for that," declared Kat. "Snacks and a possible riot consisting only of people under four feet tall. Sounds like fun."

"I don't mind going over there," noted Ellen. "I like to know what is going on at school, plus I'm interested to see how this whole second and third grade split works. You know Annie is one of the youngest ones in her class to begin with."

Kat asked, "What is that about? Again, I'm in the dark here."

"Annie is in a class that has some second graders and some third graders. It is a long story; do you remember Mrs. Rinaldi who taught high school math?" Ellen asked. "She decided that she would get her certification in elementary education and when a spot opened up, she would be able to teach in the lower grades. I think a spot only opened up because they didn't have enough kids for another second grade and another third grade, so they made it a split. None of the other teachers wanted to teach it."

Kat asked, "How did Annie end up in it?'

"Not sure, the principal called us in and asked how we felt about it, and we told him that we were fine with it," Ellen replied. "It is a small class, and this Mrs. Rinaldi is a sharp one. Any of the perks you would normally get in second grade, they get, any of the perks they would normally get in third grade, they get. Double field trip time, babies!"

Mrs. M. piped up, "Oh, so I guess you will be going to both the farm and the factory tours, bring your manure boots, Ellen."

"I don't know, I think it will be fun," Ellen remarked. "I will be helping out with the Halloween party next week and I'm bringing a scary snack."

Kat asked, "What is that like?"

"Don't know, you will have to ask my mom," Ellen explained. "She is the one making it. I think that we're supposed to dress up. For just a second, I thought about dressing like that mom with the short skirt and fishnet stockings from the pickup line at school, but I realized that would be in very poor taste not to mention hurtful. I think I will go with the standard ghost or Raggedy Ann or something."

Mrs. M. laughed, "For what it is worth I think that you would totally pull off short skirt and fishnet stockings costume but of course you have to know your audience, and these are seven-year-olds."

"They are pretty innocent at that age," noted Kat. "It is probably best to stay wholesome. What is Annie going to be?"

Ellen laughed, "She wants to be a historical figure like Amelia Earhart or a box of cereal."

"Well, that gives you something to work with for sure," Kat noted. "That is quite a wide range of ideas she is working with. I guess it is something she thought up in her free time at school."

Ellen explained, "That is what I love about Mrs. Rinaldi, there is no such thing as free time. It is reading time, game time, helping time, or about five other kinds of time. Productivity is this woman's watchword. She seems to have made a strong transition from being a high school teacher."

"I like it," Mrs. M. remarked. "Did she say why she wanted to teach in the lower grades rather than in high school?"

Ellen signed, "When we were in for conferences, I asked that, and she told us in a sort of sarcastic tone that second graders rarely have liquor on their breath in class or unplanned pregnancies."

"Well, if they did, that would be a real problem," Mrs. M. agreed.

CHAPTER 10

Mrs. Grebe's Cat, Mr. Whiskers

We were closing in on Halloween and the coffee shop was decorated with all sorts of whimsical black cats and such. It smelled like spice and cinnamon and sugar and was warm and cozy on a very cool day. Ellen and Mrs. M. were already seated, and Kat came in just behind me. She stopped at the front counter and picked up a cinnamon roll sample. Kat was also carrying a large bag with her.

Once Kat got to the table, she stood next to Ellen and pulled a child-sized white dress with a sash out of the bag. She noted "Your mom knew that I would be seeing you, so she gave this to me to give to you. She told me that she has all your old costumes in the attic and thought that you might like this Princess Diana one for your daughter this year." Kat then took a child-sized crown out of the bag and asked, "Does this look familiar?"

"Apparently, we're talking some sort of lifelong obsession with the royal family, I knew that there was something to this King Charles thing," stated Mrs. M.

Ellen defended herself, saying, "I don't even think that is my costume, it could belong to Rachel."

"I think not," noted Kat as she took a photo out of the bag clearly showing Ellen dressed as Princess

Diana. Kat added, "As a mom and homemaker your mother keeps excellent records."

Ellen sighed, "I'm giving up."

"Giving up or fessing up?" asked Mrs. M as she started setting up the walls for the Mah Jongg game.

Ellen declared, "Both, let's consider this topic closed. I have a question for Kat anyway. Do you know if your landlady has a new tenant lined up once you move out of your apartment? My brother-in-law, Bill is hoping to transfer up here to be closer to his parents and he will need a place to live."

"Is it just him?" asked Kat. "It is a cozy place, but small."

Ellen replied, "Yes. And he is really a good guy, very quiet and reliable. He works full time and doesn't have any noisy or strange hobbies that I know about."

"So, is he coming up here temporarily or is he going to relocate? I'm only asking because I think that the landlady, Mrs. Grebe will inquire," asked Kat.

Ellen noted, "I think he is most likely going to want to stay up here. He is really close to his nephews and niece. In fact, he had the kids for a week over the summer when they went to Zoo Camp. This is the cute thing that he did, he had the boys pose in the same way that he and Dean posed for photos when they were young. In one picture my boys looked so much like Dean and Bill that it almost made me cry. Then he took the two photos and put them in a side-by-side frame. He made a copy for his mom and dad too."

"So is he one of those sensitive guys?" asked Kat.

Ellen laughed, "He is just a regular guy. You know men they are simple creatures. You feed them, give them a warm place to sleep and a treat once in a while and you are all set."

"Now you sound like he is a cat or something," Mrs. M. stated.

Ellen replied, "Actually, he is a dentist and a human."

"In that case, I can talk to the landlady I don't think that she was looking forward to finding someone to rent it to. She is older and not computer savvy. She will probably be relieved," noted Kat. "There are just a few little quirky things involved in living there, like making sure that Mrs. Grebe feeds her cat, Mr. Whiskers, then bringing in the trash cans, and if he ever has pizza, Mrs. Grebe would like one slice."

Mrs. M. stated, "You had me until you got to the pizza part."

"She has acid reflux; she can't eat more than one piece," explained Kat. "I have been giving her one piece of pizza every time I buy it since I moved in there ten years ago."

Mrs. M. laughed, "You are really a stick-with-it kind of woman, aren't you Kat?"

"Why do you think that she has never raised the rent?" replied Kat.

CHAPTER 11

Riot Recap

I was the first one to get to the coffee shop and it was warm and welcoming. I did notice a small but beautiful wedding cake on display. It seemed an odd time of year to get married, but the cake itself was breathtaking in detail. I went up to the counter to get a sample of strudel and mentioned to the owner that the cake was beautiful. She in turn called to the back and had the baker come out so I could tell him in person.

He seemed extremely happy to hear a nice comment about his work. In a slight European accent, he said "You know the bride, she gave me an idea, and I made something that I thought that she would love." I told him that I was sure that the bride would love it and that he did a wonderful job. He held up a finger to indicate that I should wait a minute and went to the back. He came out with a piece of cake. "This is the same cake I made for the bride, it is a light cherry with almond, I keep a few pieces back in the bakery to eat because it is so good. I hope that you like it." I thanked him profusely and went to the Mah Jongg table.

As soon as Kat came in, I told her the story and split the cake with her. Of course, she was thrilled and remarked that she would consider that flavor for one of her upcoming wedding cakes. We scarfed it down before Mrs. M. or Ellen got there and they were none the wiser about our little cake caper.

Once the others got there, we started to play. Kat asked how Ellen's stint as room mother went and she told us it was indeed a near riot. Ellen said, "For one I would not recommend bobbing for apples. We did a trial run before the kids got there and it was a watery mess, so we just cut up the apples and called it a snack. The other parent and I were laughing so hard we could not contain ourselves."

Kat asked, "How were the kids? Were there any meltdowns or the like?"

"They were pretty well-behaved," noted Ellen. "There was this one little imp who kept trying to get more candy. There were also a couple of wardrobe malfunctions. No one likes being stuck by a pin and many of the costumes were held together with pins. There were a few tears, and one little girl got upset because no one could guess what her costume was supposed to be. I could not figure it out either. Interestingly enough, Annie guessed it right away."

Mrs. M. asked, "What did Annie end up wearing?"

"She was a box of cereal, and it was so cute," stated Ellen. "Dean brought home a box from work and one of his guys had done artwork on it, so it looked like a real box of cereal. The art was excellent. I asked Dean if the guy was an artist. Dean said, 'no, he is an electrician,' which for some reason was funny to me. I had Annie write him a thank you note even though my husband told me it wasn't necessary since he worked on it while he was on the clock."

Kat noted, "It is good to get them in the habit of writing a little note as a thank you. I try to always remember to do that."

"Well, what she wanted to do was to wrap up a box of that kind of cereal and include it with the note," Ellen said. "I thought that was funny but a little over the top."

Kat asked, "So overall the party went ok, over at the school then?"

"There was a bit of a mini riot when the kids went outside for a fire drill," explained Ellen. "I would like to state that the day of the Halloween Party is not the day to do a fire drill but whatever. They were doing fine until suddenly out of nowhere it started to rain hard. Due to wearing costumes no one had coats on and there was this giant rush towards the doors. Of course, some people were tripping over their wings or light sabers or whatever else they had with them or were wearing. By the time we got it all sorted out we had an entire class of wet kids and two scraped knees."

Mrs. Rinaldi looked at me and said, "This is much better than them coming in from a fire drill smelling like pot."

"She is definitely on to something there," stated Mrs. M.

CHAPTER 12

Baby Jail

Molly was already seated when I walked into the coffee shop and gave me a big smile as I sat down. She started by saying, "I know that we were introduced, I'm Molly."

I reminded her that my name was Darcy, and I told her that I had heard that she was an excellent Mah Jongg Player. She laughed and noted, "I really like playing for some reason. I didn't think that it would be for me, I'm more of an outdoor person. I like to walk and skate and the like, but Mah Jongg appeals to my inner nerd, I think. It really is a thinking person's game. Plus, you can't beat the company. I just love the group so much."

"I agree," I stated. "I like this little group too. Everyone has a sense of humor, which works for me."

Molly asked, "Do you live around her? Someone told me you work at the college."

"Yes, on both counts," I confirmed. "In terms of being able to substitute for Mah Jongg my schedule is flexible until it isn't."

Molly replied, "I know exactly what you mean. I'm not sure that you are aware of it, but this group was always Mrs. M., Ellen, Mrs. M's sister Martha and me for years. Once in a great while Lisa or Alexis would substitute. Martha died suddenly and Mrs. M. did not want to continue playing. She had lost her husband a few years earlier and she took both deaths hard."

"That is awful," I remarked. "How did you get her to change her mind?'

Molly went on, "We recruited Kat to be our new player and when Mrs. M. did not show up here to play, we went over to her house. Mrs. M. is a strong person, but she seemed to be at her breaking point. Kat was really the one who turned it around. Before you knew it, we were all laughing and talking and the next week playing Mah Jongg back here. I always feel like we all have a little magic in us and this time it was Kat who was able to bring it out."

"You are making me happy just hearing that story," I remarked. "You never really know when you are going to make an impact on someone."

Molly explained, "You know Mrs. M. is a little aloof and apart from people, but she means really well. She knitted over twenty little hats for me when I told her the kids at my friend's school were under-dressed last winter. She dismissed it like it was noth-ing, that is how she is. From what I hear she seems to have taken to you right away. That is quite a feat, I can tell you from personal experience."

I laughed, "That is good to know. My sister told me not to win too much and not to talk too much so I have been following that advice. I enjoy people that have lively conversations, so this is easy for me."

"Oh my gosh, yes," Molly noted. "Sometimes I just laugh and laugh. I'm not that much of an outgoing person, but they bring out my sense of humor too. I know when I was with the group earlier, I said something about Ellen's sister telling secrets about Ellen. I wondered if I was out of line, but Ellen just laughed. I worry too much about what other people think."

I responded, "That is a human condition, especially for women."

"I know," said Molly. "Getting back to Mrs. M., I have never known how to thank her for all she did for me when I had a reoccurrence of my cancer last year. Mrs. M. was with me at the hospital, and she brought me food all the time when I was recovering. She just kept saying that it was nothing, but it meant a lot to me. Ellen's sister Rachel is the same way."

Just then Kat came in the door, she stopped at the front of the bakery and picked up a free sample. Once she got to the table she sat down.

"What are we talking about?" asked Kat.

I replied, "You know the usual, girl talk."

"I just stopped by and saw Alexis's babies, and they are so cute," noted Kat. "She looked good too. She has promised to bring her big old double baby stroller over here someday and show them off. Alexis told me that they have only been mistaken for her grandchildren three times lately."

Molly added directing her comments to me, "She is 46 years old or something like that and has a good sense of humor."

"She is going to need it, once those kids start to move around on their own it is going to be non-stop for her," remarked Kat. "I know she got a baby jail at the shower."

"Play-pen?" Molly asked.

Kat answered, "I like to call it the baby jail. You know babies, they are always guilty of something. You can detain them indefinitely if you have any suspicions, maybe they pulled the cat's tail or got into the cookie drawer."

"With two of them there is no telling," stated Molly.

Ellen came in and had her own Mah Jongg set with her. We sat down to play, and she asked how everyone was doing. Ellen said, "There was a bit of a fracas in the pickup line at school the other day."

"What happened? Molly asked.

Ellen went on, "It was nice out and we were all standing around. I'm sure I have mentioned the fishnet stocking, short skirt wearing mom Trixie. She was just standing there along with the other moms and one dad, Reverend Bob. All of a sudden, this giant rough looking guy jumps out of a truck and walks up to her and starts yelling. I saw him raise his hand to her and out of nowhere Reverend Bob grabbed the guy and put him in a headlock. It was over very fast."

"Oh my gosh, did the kids see it?" I asked.

Ellen explained, "No luckily, they were not out yet. The guards came rushing up and took him away. A few minutes later I could see a police car on the other side of the school."

"Wow," I said.

Ellen added, "I didn't realize that Reverend Bob had it in him. I have a lot of respect for that guy.

The last I looked over there he and this Trixie were talking, and he was calming her down."

"That was quite a thing to see," Molly said. "After that story, I think that I need a little snack to get ready for Mah Jongg."

Kat mentioned that there were samples of muffins at the front of the shop. "No cake?" asked Ellen.

"You guys know that I always say that brownies are cake's cousin, I wonder what muffins are to cake?" asked Molly.

Kat stated definitively, "Uncle." Everyone chuckled and started playing.

CHAPTER 13

Runaway Turkeys

It had been a few weeks since I played Mah Jongg, and it was a very cold and blustery day. Winter was right around the corner. I was surprised to see Ellen, Mrs. M. and Kat were already there even though I was on time.

Everyone had a heavy coat hanging on their chair, except of course Mrs. M., whose full-length camel hair coat was characteristically folded gracefully over a chair on another table.

The group greeted me warmly and asked how my plans were coming for Thanksgiving. I mentioned that I had been at the grocery store and there was a huge sign that read, "DO NOT ATTEMPT TO PUT TURKEYS ON THE CONVEYER, LEAVE THEM IN YOUR CART." I asked them what they thought of that.

Mrs. M. noted, "I saw that sign too. What do you think happened there? I'm thinking that a turkey was placed on the conveyer and somehow the conveyer sped up and shot the turkey off the end and hit the packer or the like. What else could it be?"

"I wanted to ask, but sometimes it is best not to know," I commented.

Ellen chimed in, "I always love shopping the day

48

before Thanksgiving and seeing these people with a 25-pound plus rock-hard, frozen turkey in their cart. Like they are going to thaw that baby out in one day. I also take issue with people who attempt to make a pie or something for the first time for an important holiday. I think I have made my feelings about who can and cannot bake very clear."

Everyone laughed. Mrs. M. leaned over towards me and stated, "Ellen is not always the best arbiter of who is a good baker and who is not. Funny story, Ellen was so sure that some mom at the school pickup line, I believe her name was Trixie would not be able to bake cookies, and this woman ended up bringing the best cookies to the bake sale. Ellen had to eat her words so to speak."

Ellen noted, "In my defense, the woman in question wore fishnet stockings, low-cut shirts, and short skirts every day to the pick-up line at the elementary school. Imagine my surprise when she came in with some great cookies."

"Could you tell that they were homemade? You know sometimes people try to pass off bakery cookies as their own," said Kat.

Ellen signed and said, "I asked her some rather pointed questions about the cookies trying to ascertain if she did actually bake them. The next time she saw me she gave me a copy of the recipe with handwritten notes. I own my misjudgment."

"What were the cookies like?" asked Kat.

Mrs. M. remarked, "So out of this whole story you are interested in what the cookies tasted like?"

"That and this whole, don't take the turkey out of the cart," Kat responded. "What if it is a small turkey? What is the cut-off?"

Ellen noted directing her question towards Kat, "Speaking of Thanksgiving, you will be at my parents' place for the holiday, yes?"

"Sadly no," Kat shared. "I'm working a twelve-hour shift. I traded away my Thanksgiving earlier this year, not realizing that I would be engaged and actually have plans other than feeding Mrs. Grebe's cat this year. Things change fast."

Ellen laughed, "That is for sure, apparently Uncle Stan has other plans as well. He said something about not being in Michigan for the holiday. Do you know anything about that Mrs. M?" Ellen leaned over to me and noted, "Mrs. M. and my Uncle Stan are let's just say 'keeping company' and she is very cagey about it."

Kat bailed Mrs. M. out by saying, "I think that I may be able to get over to your folks' house by about 7:30 pm so at least I will be there for desserts. I heard that your mom is making four different pies."

"Kat bringing up desserts, I can't say that I'm surprised," remarked Ellen.

CHAPTER 14

Return of the Walking Ruckus

It was full on late fall by the next time I substituted for Mah Jongg. The leaves were scattered by blowing winds and it was quite chilly for early December in Michigan. I heard on the news that they had ten inches of snow in the Upper Peninsula. I wore my warm coat and realized that my second thoughts about wearing boots were definitely right. By the time I scooted into the coffee shop I was quite chilled. Kat and Ellen were already there eating pastry samples and laughing up a storm. Ellen asked me how my trip to Sarasota went.

I said, "It was the same general routine when we visit. Out to dinner, buy groceries for her and go for walks. I did however, go to a very quaint antique shop and found you this wonderful cup with Prince Charles's face on it." I pulled the mug out of my bag and gave it to Ellen.

Ellen laughed and said almost sarcastically, "It is a classic, from before he was King. I will cherish it forever and I WILL remember who gave it to me. Someone I thought I could count on NOT to be in on this particular joke."

"I couldn't help myself," I stated. "It was sitting there all alone on the shelf among mugs that said stuff like, 'best grandma in the world' and 'I left my heart in El Paso' and I just had to rescue poor Prince Charles and bring him to someone who would truly appreciate him."

Ellen laughed, "I do appreciate it. I think that I am warming up to the whole collection thing. Before you know it I will be one of those people who has a whole room devoted to ceramic cats or Elvis dolls."

I laughed and sat down next to Ellen. She turned to me and asked, "Have you seen the new version of the commercial that Kat is in? They put one out last spring but now they are doing print ads and even a mailer. The new version of the commercial shows her walking down this long hallway and there is talking over it."

I replied, "I have seen the commercial, but I didn't get the mailer. I think that I live too far out of town for that. What does the mailer look like?"

"Let me put it to you this way," explained Kat. "My face is on the front of the mailer. In fact, my face is the whole front of the mailer. To make it even worse, I was at the post office and there were like twenty copies of the mailer people had gotten in their mailboxes and then thrown in the trash. It is quite an uneasy feeling seeing a trash can full of pictures of your face."

I observed, "I bet that would be traumatic. The commercial is good though. Did it take a long time to shoot?"

"Funny you asked," replied Kat. "They kept asking me to walk slower, walk faster, look down, look up and on and on. They probably filmed that same hallway in twenty different ways. That hallway is nowhere near my area, but you would only know that if you worked at the hospital. The director kept telling me to walk faster and at one point he told me to run. I made a face and told him, 'If I'm doing my job correctly, I don't need to run because I have everything organized and under control.' He laughed hard and told me that I was a firecracker."

Ellen asked, "Firecracker? I'm surprised he didn't call you a walking ruckus. That would definitely be appropriate for the situation. I saw the commercial and you look serious yet friendly. It is a good thing that you didn't have to wear a mask and try to smile with your eyes. That may have been a bridge too far. Remind me again, why were you expected to do these ads again? You had your turn. Did you miss a meeting again and get volunteered?"

"This is confidential," stated Kat quietly, "but the person from our department that they had scheduled to do it just got so nervous that they couldn't use her footage. She is in the background in one shot, but she just got too worked up that she couldn't do it. I volunteered to step in. It was one of those things where I heard myself saying that I would do it and I couldn't believe that it came out of my mouth."

I laughed, "That is how I got roped into teaching 'Literature Through Film' last semester. I heard myself saying I would do it and just could not believe that I did."

"I thought I was the only one that did that," Ellen commented. "I ended up leading a workshop where only a handful of the participants spoke English. I believe that none of the full-time people would take it but I had told them I would be willing to fill in any Wednesday morning and now I'm wondering if they scheduled it so I would have to do it."

Kat remarked, "Now I'm wondering if that girl really wasn't nervous and messed up the commercial on purpose."

"I'm beginning to have my doubt about that 'Literature Through Film' class now that we're talking about it," I noted.

As the three of us sat there, contemplating what we had just heard and said, Mrs. M. walked in and asked what we were talking about. Ellen shared, "Mostly questioning the life choices that we are making and wondering if we have inadvertently been lured into bottom of the barrel assignments."

"Are we talking about your workshop from last month, Senorita?" Mrs. M. asked.

Ellen noted, "Yes, and Kat making her second appearance in the hospital commercial and Darcy is teaching something called Literature Through Film which sounds like the English class equivalent of Math for Morons."

"I can't meet you ladies at the bottom of the barrel because as you know I have the ability to say no and mean it," explained Mrs. M. laughing.

Ellen noted, "Oh really. Didn't you tell me that you were bringing us each a giant tin of popcorn because you bought six of them as part of the high school band fundraiser?"

"It was seven," Mrs. M. responded. "That means seven little trombone players will be able to go to the competition in Mt. Pleasant. That is hardly bottom of the barrel."

Kat noted, "Especially if you are standing on seven tins of popcorn."

CHAPTER 15

A Long Drive Down a Dark Road

I substituted the very next week for Mrs. M. who apparently was visiting Scotland and Wales. Ellen stated, "I get all my information on her comings and goings from Uncle Stan. Yet he is very discreet on what the actual nature of their relationship is." She turned to me and asked, "As an outsider has she given you any clues about how serious they are?"

I confirmed, "No, but she does have this little smile every time his name comes up in conversation. I'm not sure if you can tell anything from that. How long has she been a widow?"

"Many, many years," answered Ellen. "I wonder about that sometimes in terms of my brother-in-law. Bill lost his wife seven or eight years ago and he is still young, and he does not seem ready to get into a relationship. We don't even try to fix him up anymore and he is cool with that. Speaking of him Kat, are you guys all ready for the apartment switcharoo?"

Kat laughed, "Yes, I have been preparing the landlady, Mrs. Grebe for the past month or so. I mentioned that he was a dentist and that seemed to impress her. I think this weekend he is bringing his stuff up here and Molly is helping me move my stuff out." Kat turned to me, "I'm moving in with my fiancé, Chuck. We decided if we lived together, we would have more time together."

"Makes sense," I stated.

Ellen added, "The timing is perfect, my brother-in-law works for one of those chain dental clinics and he had to wait for an opening at this branch. His parents are both in assisted living, and he wants to be closer to them. He knows a few people. He and Chuck have golfed when he was up here and of course my husband Dean is his brother."

Just then Lisa came in, Ellen stated "Let the interrogation begin, I wonder what Lisa knows about her mother-in-law gallivanting around Europe with Uncle Stan."

Lisa waved to everyone as she came in the door of the coffee shop. She asked, "So what is the topic, ladies?"

"My brother-in-law is moving up here from Grand Rapids, and he is moving into Kat's old apartment," Ellen responded.

Lisa asked, "That place is pretty small, isn't it Kat?"

"He is by himself," Ellen stated. "He is one of these shy guys who works a lot of hours and keeps to himself. As long as he remembers the house rules that Mrs. Grebe has, he will be fine."

Lisa turned to Kat, "Are you still her pizza dealer?"

Kat laughed, "Yes. When you put it that way, it just sounds wrong."

Lisa laughed, "It sounds funny if you asked me. Normally, it wouldn't be funny but since you have been supplying her with pizza for ten years it is plenty funny. So, your brother-in-law Ellen, is he divorced or what? Asking for a friend."

"His wife died a few years ago," answered Ellen as she set up the Mah Jongg game. "Honestly, I don't think he is even interested in meeting anyone else. He told my husband that he didn't think that he would ever find love again."

Lisa commented, "I get it, regardless my cousin moved back into town at the beginning of the school year. She is in her early 30s. I would love to see her meet someone. We could fix them up."

"Do people even do that anymore?" I asked.

Lisa answered, "I do that. My mother-in-law and Kat both met someone based on a single evening of food and slides of Italy earlier this year. I must admit I was as surprised as anyone concerning those matches. I knew Chuck's ex-finance. He dodged a bullet there. Kat, you are a hundred times better than she will ever be and you are so good for Chuck. As for Mrs. M. I thought that whole romance ship had sailed."

"It did sail, all the way over to Portugal, and now to Wales," noted Ellen. "So, do you think that they are serious? They are taking major trips together. I didn't get the impression that it was a group charter. I think it is just the two of them. I can't get a read on it. No one tells me anything."

Lisa stated, "You are not alone on that. I didn't even know that she was leaving the country until she told me that she needed me to substitute for Mah Jongg. It would be easier if she had a cat or plants to water. That way we could get into her place and look around for clues."

Ellen laughed, "I was going to interrogate you to see what you knew but apparently we both know nothing."

"Yes, we won't have any better luck with my daughters, they told me that Grandma was going to see a whale," explained Lisa. "Of course, she was actually going to Wales."

Kat noted, "You really can't count on preschoolers for accurate information. I wish that I had known that she was going to Wales. I would have asked her to buy me a commemorative plate with King Charles's face on it. Christmas is coming and I don't have anything for Ellen."

"I can only hope that you are joking," Ellen chimed in. "I thought this whole teasing me about King Charles was put to bed."

Kat laughed, "I wish that I could, but I can't because it is just so funny and so out of character for you. It makes me smile just thinking of you mooning over Charles or dressing like Princess Diana. So happy."

Ellen turned to me, "So this is what the future holds, Kat is going to marry into the family and hold this over my head for the indefinite future. You mentioned that you have a sister, Darcy. Has this ever happened to you?" Ellen asked, directing her question to me.

"Oh yes, bad perm, bad boyfriend, losing all my books in high school in the creek, unfortunate prom dress, not paying her back for a gift for my mom one time, taking someone else's gloves at a restaurant," I explained. "Need I go on?"

Ellen replied, "Not really. But I would like to know how you happened to take the wrong gloves."

"I'm interested in the bad perm and the unfortunate prom dress," noted Kat. "I'm assuming there are photos. Did they both happen at the same time?"

I told them, "Oh no, I believe that we have started a long drive down a dark road."

Lisa laughed and said, "I believe we have."

CHAPTER 16

Nine Fruitcakes Too Many

It was less than a week until Christmas and Mrs. M. was still "abroad" as Ellen put it. She asked me to sit in next week as well and I was happy to do so. Molly was back and apparently had swung through the southern states on a business trip. She looked quite tan and relaxed.

Ellen asked how the apartment move went. Both Kat and Molly explained that it was smooth, and that Ellen's brother-in-law Bill had brought Mrs. Grebe flowers and a toothbrush as a thank you for renting to him.

Molly mentioned, "He has good manners, and I can tell you that from what I have seen in the dating world and in life in general. You know, I just returned from the south and there are some guys with great manners down there. My experience here in the north with men who have good manners has been spotty at best. Do you remember that guy George? He never opened a door for me in all the time that we were dating."

"Did you meet anyone on this trip?" asked Ellen.

Molly laughed and replied, "I'm working when I'm on the road and there is not much time for that sort of thing. Plus, right now I think that I'm just going to work on myself and try to stay healthy."

"Great plan, I'm glad that you will be back in town until after the new year," noted Kat. "On a different topic, we're in full Christmas mode in our department. Sadly, I took a lot of heat over my Secret Santa gift, I can tell you. For years I have been known for giving out great Secret Santa gifts. This year I gave a gift certificate for an oil change at one of Chuck's dealerships, which is actually a very valuable gift. It was not well received."

Ellen asked, "Why? Did the recipient not know how to drive?"

"I think that people are used to food gifts from me, you know due to my, shall we say, inclination towards baked goods," Kat stated. "I thought that the oil change would be great, but it was a big dud. I might as well buy them a big bag of rice or toilet paper like they do in Hawaii."

I asked, "What did you get?'

"Hand-knit hat and scarf that matches my coat, lovely work," Kat answered. "Plus, one lady brought in fruit cakes for everyone. Mysteriously, most of them ended up on my desk once she went home for the day. I now have 9 fruitcakes. I left one in the break room, and I will be bringing some to your mom's house, Ellen."

"What did my mom ever do to you?" Ellen remarked laughing.

Molly interjected, "No love for the fruitcake over there?"

"You should come over and see unless you have plans," mentioned Ellen. "Your brother and Rachel have already confirmed they will be there, so where would you go since they will be with us?"

Molly smiled and said, "I guess I could think about it."

"You know we will have a whole big crowd there" Ellen said. She added, "I'm sure that you are asking yourself what my mom will be making. The answer to that is, everything."

Molly and Kat both laughed.

Kat remarked, "I'm going to be off the whole day even though I'm working a double on Christmas Eve. I will probably be in my pajamas, snuggled up with Chuck and some fruitcake."

"That is an adorable picture, for sure," Molly remarked. "On a non-Christmas related topic, what about Mrs. M., still cavorting with Uncle Stan across the ocean?"

Ellen laughed, "Yes, she is, and the mystery continues. Apparently, my next step is to contact Interpol."

"Couldn't you just send her an email wishing her Merry Christmas and find out where she is?" asked Molly.

Ellen answered, "I don't want to arouse too much suspicion."

"Oh yes, the government always tells you to be alert for Christmas greetings around Christmas time. I think I saw a bulletin about that on the State Department website," noted Kat.

Everyone including Ellen laughed and with that we started setting up the game.

CHAPTER 17

Wait, what?

_____

It was that slow week between Christmas and New Year's Day. The whole world does not know what to do with itself and the Christmas decorations are starting to sag. The coffee shop had large samples of Christmas treats out even though I personally was stuffed from Christmas itself and did not try any.

Mrs. M. was not expected and I settled in and waited for Kat, Molly and Ellen. They came in at about the same time and sat down. Kat showed off a heart necklace she received as a gift from Chuck. Ellen teased her, "Did he also give you a certificate for an oil change?"

"Funny" answered Kat. She then turned to me and remarked, "We had so much fun playing games. I don't think that I have ever done that before. Chuck and I gave Molly and Bill a run for their money on both Ticket to Ride and Risk. The food was so good, I had some of everything and then Ellen's mom packed lunches for me for three days with leftovers. It was heaven."

Ellen directed her question to me, "How was your holiday?"

"Good," I explained. "We ate a lot and went ice skating and sledding. Do you know that big hill just outside of town? We took the sled down really early Christmas morning; you must get out there while the little ones are still opening their presents, or it is too crowded," I explained. "We wore ourselves out just trudging up the hill each time, but we laughed so much it was worth it. Then we went home and cooked a big brunch. We are establishing some nice traditions"

Before we started playing Ellen pulled a pair of gloves out of her purse and handed them to Molly. Ellen noted, "Before I forget, you left these in Bill's truck." Molly took the gloves and thanked her.

In my mind, I'm thinking, wait, what? Am I the only person questioning this? Why was Molly in Bill's truck? Was something going on there? Everyone seemed to be minding their tiles, so I just tucked that piece of information away in my mind for a later time. I thought to myself this Mah Jongg table is possibly the center of the universe.

The discussion returned to New Year's Eve plans. Kat told us that she would be working on New Year's Eve. Ellen shared that she would be with her husband and kids following the tradition that her husband's family had of making predictions for the next year and reading the ones they made last year.

Ellen remarked, "It is such a crack up. When the kids were little, I'm not sure that they understood the whole thing very well and they would say things like, 'we will visit Grandma' or 'the dog will have puppies'. These days it is more of a put it out there type situation where they want something, so they try to

65

conjure it up by making a prediction. I can't wait to see what they predict for next year. In case you are interested Molly, Bill won't be with us; he is the on-call dentist since he is the newest person in the office."

"I have plans with Rachel and my brother, but thanks for the non-invitation," noted Molly laughing.

Ellen looked at me and asked, "You?"

"Four-day whirlwind trip to Sarasota to see my mother-in-law. It is a tradition and one of those things that maybe eight years ago I could not believe the words came out of my mouth, 'sure let's go down there and see your mother on New Year's Eve.' We have not spent a New Year's Eve here since then." I told them. "We leave tomorrow."

Molly noted, "I'm not sure who wins on this one for having the worse plans, Kat is working but your plans do involve a mother-in-law so that is a tough choice. At least you will have a few days of warm weather."

"I agree with that," I remarked. "I will be back for next week's game just in case Mrs. M. is still gone or someone else is gone. Still no word from the British Isles?"

Ellen laughed, "No, nothing from Interpol, I'm thinking of checking with MI-5 next."

I just shook my head.

CHAPTER 18

Mostly Bridesmaids

It was cold out and the kind of Michigan day where the wind blew relentlessly from the west and the snow was piled everywhere. Mrs. M. was still gone. I arrived early and sat sipping on tea and awaiting the arrival of the other players. Kat came in through the door, also early.

She seemed happy to see me and asked if I had a minute to chat. I patted the next chair over and nodded yes. Kat said, "You know I don't remember much about growing up, but I do remember that my mom used to pat the chair like that to get me to sit next to her."

I smiled and said, "You know my Grandma McGregor always did that. It is funny the stuff you remember. I think about her almost every day."

Kat commented, "I rarely think of anything in my past. I don't know how much you know but my dad killed my mom and sister, and he died in prison. It is a terrible story. That is why I feel like I have to say it all at once, quickly and just get it all out. At that point I felt like I was really alone in the world. Looking back, it could have gone wrong in so many ways for me. Just by chance I started to babysit for Alexis for her first set of twins. She and her husband were so great to me. They got me thinking about college and a career and making something of my life. They included me in so many parts of their family life, saying that they needed me to watch the boys. You know Alexis bought me the first new winter coat I ever had."

Kat looked a little like she might cry but she held it together. "You know, I have heard nothing but good things about Alexis," I said as I patted Kat's arm.

"Oh yes, she is the best," Kat said. "Actually, that leads me to what I wanted to talk to you about. I need to bounce this off someone that I'm not potentially related to."

"Go on," I told her.

"We're working on our wedding planning," Kat explained. "I'm at a point where I'm not making progress. You know my fiancé Chuck's ex left him three days before their wedding. It was all set up and all the planning that went into it was over the top. Now that we're going to get married, it seems like all the things we talk about planning bring up bad memories for him. I want some of those things, but I respect his feelings."

"Like what?" I asked.

Kat answered, "I would like a bridal party with people dressed alike, pictures, and a cake. The issue is he had this whole big production planned with her and it is just painful for him to go through it again. I'm at a loss."

"Can you focus on exactly what you want and only do those things? I asked.

Kat asked, "I could but can I have my wedding

just be thirteen people three of whom are dressed like bridesmaids?"

"Of course you can," I answered. "You are the bride; all bets are off. Would you be able to have a very small ceremony with just immediate family, perhaps at someone's home? I'm talking just the bridal party and parents. You could have the ceremony, take photos, eat cake and then in the summer have a big party for everyone you know. We did something like that."

Kat stated excitedly, "Oh my gosh, that would solve so many problems. Plus, it is Ellen's dream to have her and her sister Rachel wear matching bridesmaid dresses. I could get some Hawaiian summer looking dresses for them, and Molly too."

"There you go, what about groomsmen, do you have guys who would go along with that?" I asked. "You want your photos to be balanced."

Kat laughed, "My two new brothers-in-law and maybe Bill. They could wear white shirts and khakis. That would be a great look with the Hawaiian bridesmaid dresses. We could take loads of pictures or even hire a photographer. I think that I want a wedding dress like my friend had last spring in Hawaii, which I could wear again for the big party in the summer. I could do a whole Hawaiian theme. This is so great. It will be so different from Chuck's other wedding. Of course, I will need cakes for both events."

"Of course, cake is a given. Do you need someone to perform the ceremony?" I asked. "You probably remember, my sister is a judge. She would probably do it." I added. "She works for cake."

Kat laughed, "I'm going to run all this by Chuck and see how he feels about it. I can't believe that I have been wrestling with this forever, and we sat down and just figured it out just like that."

I told her that I was happy to help. I mentioned, "When I was working on my degree. I had all these notes for my thesis. I just could not get into the zone to even flesh out my writing, let alone write the thesis. I was stuck in an airport for a four-hour layover, and I just started working on it. By the time they called my plane, I had an outline and a great start on the actual writing. I was in the zone."

Kat observed, "We were in that same zone today. I'm so excited about my plans but please don't mention anything we talked about. I want to talk to Chuck about it before I break it to Ellen and Molly that there are matching Hawaiian dresses of my choice in their future."

"Of course, and let me know if you want to go forward so I can ask my sister about presiding," I told her.

Kat nodded, "You really could not have been more help today. I can't wait to talk to Chuck."

"Just to review, what is the most important thing that you want at your wedding?" I asked.

Kat responded immediately, "Chuck."

I laughed "That is the right answer."

Kat laughed, "You know I almost said cake."

"I know that you did," I noted, and we both laughed.

Just then Ellen and Molly came into the shop. They sat down and asked what we were talking about. Kat piped up, "The weather, it has been so windy."

"On another topic, Mrs. M. apparently flew back in yesterday," Ellen stated. "I'm getting all my information from Uncle Stan these days via my mom. We will have to interrogate Mrs. M. if she plays next week."

Kat laughed, "All I can say is, good luck with that. She is a vault. I found out from the band teacher that she did indeed buy seven tins of popcorn as well as new band uniforms for the whole brass section. She neglected to mention that part of the story to us."

"She will probably just say that it is nothing and then start talking about the weather," added Ellen.

Kat did her best impression of Mrs. M., saying, "It was nothing. It has been so chilly, don't you think?"

Then Kat kicked my shin under the table, and I added, "Yes, unseasonably chilly." Everyone nodded and we started to play.

CHAPTER 19

Bye-bye Bertha

I arrived early at the coffee shop and stopped at the front counter to pick up a wonderful cream filled puff that melted in my mouth. I sat drinking tea and thinking about how I was fitting in with the other Mah Jongg players. I thought that I had been a help to Kat in planning her wedding and I wondered if she decided to use any of the ideas we talked about.

It was so cold and windy out that any thoughts of upcoming warm weather events were welcome. Everyone agreed that it had been a particularly bad winter but that didn't do anything to make it better. I was substituting for Mrs. M., but I didn't know the reason for her absence.

Ellen and Kat arrived together and sat down. Ellen pulled out her Mah Jongg set and started to build the walls while Kat went to the front counter to get a pastry sample and coffee. I asked Ellen how things were going for her, and she laughed. "I have to say there are times when you just have to marvel at things," she said.

"How so?" I asked.

Ellen replied, "For one thing, the other day I was at the pickup line for school waiting for Annie. It was cold out, so I was waiting in the car. Once the kids came out, I noticed that Trixie, you know the one who dresses slutty but makes good cookies, was waiting in Reverend Bob's vehicle. When the kids came out, she popped out of the front seat, short skirt and all."

"What do you think?" I asked. "They are acquainted, didn't he keep her ex from hitting her earlier this year or something like that? Maybe it was a little thank you conversation or maybe they had to discuss strategy for whatever trial they may both have to testify at."

Ellen remarked, "I should have known that is the way that your mind works with your family being judges and lawyers. I honestly had not thought of that. My mind went to shenanigans because that's how my mind works."

Kat sat down and asked, "What are you saying about how your mind works? I would be very interested to be able to get inside there and see what is actually going on most of the time. I think that it would be fascinating."

"It is a deep, dark place," Ellen remarked. "You do not want to go there. Trust me, you are better off with your sunny disposition and thinking that most people are like you."

Kat noted, "You know you and my future husband both share the same parents and upbringing. And let's not even get started on Rachel. There's lots to analyze there. I have spent hours thinking about what she is thinking. I have a whole portion of my brain dedicated to trying to figure the two of you sisters out."

"I wouldn't spend lots of time on that," Ellen said

chuckling. "You have a wedding coming up so your focus should be on establishing what the rest of your life is going to be like. Chuck said something to me about getting rid of your car."

Kat commented, "Not that, my PT cruiser is sacred. It was the first new vehicle I ever bought. I love it so much."

"Do you love it more than Chuck?" Ellen asked. "You know that you are going to be the new first lady of transportation in this town. The guy who owns the other two big dealerships, his wife is not in the picture, so it is up to you now. You can't drive a car that is that old if you are the queen of the dealerships, can you?"

Kat remarked, "Now that you put it that way, I guess I can let Bertha go."

"Your PT Cruiser is named Bertha?" I asked.

Kat smiled and said, "Yes, the lady at the bank who approved me for the loan was named Bertha. She did me a solid, so I named the car after her."

"You are going to have to run all future vehicle names past me," Ellen stated. Just then Molly came in. Ellen explained that Kat was going to have to get rid of her PT Cruiser.

Molly exclaimed, "Not Bertha. We went to Canada so many times in that car. It was the best. We brought that big chair home in it one time. Why, why, why?"

"Apparently I'm going to be the first lady of transportation in this town once I marry Chuck," Kat explained. "Bertha is not coming along for the ride."

Molly said, "So I guess you are willing to social

climb your way right over Bertha."

"I have no choice," Kat said. "Sacrifices need to be made."

Ellen added, "Chuck said you could have a sports-car."

"Goodbye Bertha," Kat replied.

CHAPTER 20

Don't tell the Tooth Fairy

I was surprised to get a call to substitute in the Mah Jongg group. It had been several weeks since I last played, and I knew that Mrs. M. had returned from her trip. I was anxious to see who showed up for the game. Mrs. M. was already there when I arrived at the coffee shop. Ellen and Kat came in soon after. Kat of course picked up a sample of cake from the front counter. It was a very cold winter day, and everyone was wearing heavy coats. Mrs. M. looked the same as she usually did, classy and sharp.

We were seated and I asked Mrs. M. how her trip was. She laughed and stated, "I was thinking that you were going to wish me a Happy New Year." She gestured towards Ellen, "This one, will tell you Happy New Year in July if she hasn't seen you since the start of the year."

I responded, "Happy New Year. I hope that you had a great trip."

"Did Uncle Stan have a nice time?" Ellen probed.

Mrs. M. responded, "Oh yes, you know he was the one who insisted that we pick up that King Charles dishtowel set for you. I hope that you will cherish it forever. It is so classy and refined and will go with the mug that Kat bought in Bermuda."

Sensing perhaps that Mrs. M. was not going to be forthcoming, Ellen remarked, "Speaking of travel, the guys are all going down to Grand Rapids for the Griffins game next week. My husband was wondering if any of us wanted to go. Personally, I'm not seeing it. I think it will be both of our dads, Dean, my boys, Chuck, Bill, Uncle Stan and Rachel's husband."

The ladies all nodded no. Not a hockey fan in the bunch, I thought to myself. In my mind, I was also thinking that I have been involved with these ladies for over a year, and I have yet to see Rachel and her husband has never been named. He is always referred to as Rachel's husband. Another Mah Jongg mystery that I have yet to solve.

Ellen continued, "Bill did some emergency dental work for a couple of the players last year and they stayed in touch. He can get tickets when he wants them. I'm not a big fan, but my boys are super excited. It might be a fun night for an all-girls Lunar New Year party."

Kat turned to me, "Oh yes, Lunar New Year. Darcy, you mentioned that you had a place in Kauai for several years, is that why you are up on the whole Lunar New Year thing?"

"Oh yes, I have already ordered my red envelopes," I told them.

"Really," noted Ellen. "It is hard to believe that there is another person in Missaukee County who celebrates Lunar New Year."

I laughed and noted, "I would not call it a celebration, I usually just send envelopes to my Hawaii

77

friends with a dollar in each and for my friends here, I put in lottery tickets or a chap stick or the like. Now if we were actually in Hawaii if would be a whole day thing."

"That was my experience too," Kat stated. "I think it is an interesting coincidence that we both have a connection to Hawaii."

I told them, "I have been called the queen of coincidence in the past. Speaking of coincidence, I did want to mention to you that I see that they are still running that commercial from the hospital. In fact, one night your commercial was on right after Chuck's commercial. You are media darlings, you two!"

"Yours is nice Kat, you are looking concerned, yet friendly in that white coat," commented Mrs. M. "Chuck's new commercial is just adorable, with the dog on the sled. Rufus is as photogenic as ever."

Ellen declared, "That dog should wear a little sign that says, 'I will work for dog treats' because I think that Chuck is going to continue to use him in his commercials for an indefinite period of time."

"Maybe Mrs. Grebe's cat Mr. Whiskers would like to do a cameo sometime, I'm pretty sure Mr. Whiskers would also work for cat treats," noted Kat. "By the way, Mrs. Grebe love, love, loves Bill. I stopped by with cake for her the other day and she went on and on. How is he settling in?"

Ellen replied, "He is doing great. It is good for us; we don't feel pressure to go see Dean and Bill's parents in the assisted living place as much. In addition to frequent visits, Bill takes his mom flowers every other week, he says that he wants the staff to know that they have people who care about them."

"Aww," stated Kat. "I did notice flowers at Mrs. Grebe's place. I wonder if Bill brought those over for her?"

Ellen replied, "That seems to be his vibe, he gives gifts of flowers and dental supplies. He is not the most inventive guy, but he is good-hearted. My little girl asked if he knew the Tooth Fairy and he told her yes. She asked him to put in a good word for her. Then she leaned over and whispered to him, 'I wasn't the one who let Rufus play in the mud, but the Tooth Fairy may have *thought* it was me.' He assured her that she was square with the Tooth Fairy."

Mrs. M. noted, "That is pretty funny. Darcy, I'm not sure if you know this, but Rufus is Ellen's dog who is frequently used in Chuck's commercials. That being said, who did let Rufus out?"

"I'm pretty sure we now know," answered Ellen as we finished up the game and started packing up. "It was weeks ago, I guess she was carrying that around with her for a while."

Once we packed up, Kat and Ellen put on their coats and started out the door. Mrs. M. was adjusting her scarf and as I started to leave the coffee shop, she gently tugged on my coat sleeve. She shared, "I didn't want to say in front of Ellen and Kat, but I will probably not be here for six to eight weeks so don't be surprised if you are asked to play."

I nodded. Mrs. M. continued, "Don't say anything to anyone but it is kind of serious, lung cancer. I'm not mentioning it to my daughter-in-law, Lisa either since she worries. Stan knows and both of my sons but that is it." She adjusted her collar and remarked lightly, "You can always text me with any gossip. I have my eye on that whole Bill and Molly situation, and I can tell that you do too."

"If Bill shows up at Mah Jongg, you will be the first to know," I told her in an effort to keep the conversation light.

Mrs. M. smiled, "That a girl."

CHAPTER 21

The Lab Coat

It was the week after Valentine's Day, and the coffee shop was already shifting into spring mode. I have to say that they were more optimistic than I was when it came to the weather in Northern Michigan in late February.

Mrs. M. was not expected, and I was substituting in her place. Ellen and Kat came in at the same time, followed by Molly whose face was red from the cold. Molly sat down and turned to Ellen, "I cannot wait to hear how the Valentine's Party at school went."

Ellen laughed, "Oh my gosh, it was the cutest thing ever. Of course, a few people throw up anytime there is excessive sugar involved but all in all a fun time. Part of the day was cutting out valentines and writing on them to take home to the parents and siblings. Then there were games and then snacks. They always say that kids say strange things, but this particular party brought out some really odd comments."

"Like what?" Molly inquired.

Ellen responded, "First you should know that the other room 'mother' was Reverend Bob, I'm sure that I have talked about him, I see him in the school pickup line often. So, he showed up and I asked him if his wife was coming and he had this real sad look and told me, 'She left me two years ago.' That was more information than I needed to hear but he was really patient with the kids and overall did a good job. He didn't seem put off by the vomiting after the snack portion of the program."

"Ick," I said. "What kind of Valentines did they end up making?"

Ellen noted "They were nice, the standard heart with words on it. There seem to be some eye-hand coordination issues with some of the second graders but the ones Annie made were cut right on the line. She finished hers up pretty fast and did some 'helping time' as Mrs. Rinaldi calls it with some of the other kids. I think the words 'hot mess' come to mind when I looked at the finished products some of these kids made. If you don't put those stick-on googly eyes in the right place, they just look creepy."

"Funny," noted Kat.

Ellen continued, "One kid wrote on a Valentine, 'I love you, but I don't like you' which was insightful but sort of tragic. Kat you will be interested to know that Annie was making a Valentine for her uncle, and I asked if she knew how to spell Chuck and she said, 'It is for Uncle Bill, he is my favorite now.' We probably should not tell Chuck or Rachel's husband about that."

As she said that I turned towards Molly to see the look on her face and Molly laughed a little because she knew what was coming from the ever-probative Ellen

Right on time, Ellen asked, "So Molly, if you had

to pick a favorite, who would it be?"

Molly stated, "Well I guess I will have to know what Kat received for Valentine's Day from Chuck before I can answer that question."

"It was romantic," remarked Kat. "This is our first Valentine's Day together so we both made an effort to make it special."

Ellen asked, "Did he spell out Happy Valentine's Day in the snow using spark plugs or something like that?"

"No," Kat replied. "That would be a waste of perfectly good spark plugs. He made me a nice dinner and then even though it was cold we made a fire outside in the fire pit and had s'mores."

Molly remarked, "I have to say he knows the way to your heart is through your stomach, as the old saying goes. I think a better question would be what did you do for him?"

"Considering that I'm a lady," Kat explained. "All I can tell you is that I met him at the door when he got home in my white lab coat."

Molly asked, "And?"

"Just the lab coat," Kat replied.

CHAPTER 22

Be on the Lookout for Rachel

Just as she had stated prior Mrs. M. was not at Mah Jongg. No one seemed to think anything of it. Molly was back and looked sharp in a turquoise coat and matching hat. Ellen asked where she got it and Molly said that she had a meeting downstate and found the coat and hat in a little boutique near Lansing. Of course, the rest of us showed up in fashion that I can only describe as 'sick of winter' which meant puffy coats and short boots. Lucky for us, the weather was breaking a little, the sun was shining and there was no new snow in sight.

Kat leaned over to me and noted, "All the wheels are in motion for an early summer wedding. We're close to working out the date. As soon as I get it, I can text it to you if it is still okay for your sister to help us out."

"Sure," I replied. "I was thinking that if she is busy there are several other judges who owe her a favor. No matter what the date is, I can get you someone."

Kat declared, "You are the best!" Kat turned to Ellen and Molly and remarked, "Darcy is going to help me get a judge for the wedding. She helped me with the planning a few weeks ago."

"Oh boy," remarked Ellen. "You better hope that

you never run into my sister Rachel. She said yes through gritted teeth about wearing this really cute bridesmaid dress. If she knew that you were responsible, she might hunt you down at your house."

Molly remarked, "I love that dress, and it looks good on all of us. Plus, we can wear it again, it is just a cute dress. Just to be safe, Darcy, we will not mention your name to Rachel."

"Honestly," I noted. "I have heard a lot about Rachel, but I could not pick her out of a lineup if my life depended upon it."

Kat laughed, "Imagine a sassier, yet more serious version of Ellen with emerald eyes. Speaking of weddings, Darcy, you never did tell me about your wedding."

"We were married in Kauai on the beach at a condo I owned at the time," I explained. "It was just us and the judge. The daytime cleaning crew was still working so they came down for the ceremony. Then they clocked out and were gone. The night security crew and property manager came and ate cake with us."

Molly remarked, "Sounds fun and very low key."

"It was. All week the staff kept coming by to get some cake," I explained. "On our actual wedding day, the property manager gave us a bottle of champagne, and we took it down to the ocean and sat on a rock and drank it and talked. Very romantic. The next day we went to Sears and bought a new refrigerator because the one at the condo died. Very traditional."

Ellen laughed, "That is pretty funny."

"It was the oddest thing," I told them. "My husband told me that he knew he wanted to marry me on our second date. I wasn't really sure until we headed down to the beach with the judge. I thought that marriage would be really hard, but it turns out it has been easy for us. I don't even know why I had a moment of doubt about it."

Kat chimed in, "It is a big decision. I think people sometimes take it too lightly and sometimes too seriously. What is it your mom always says, Ellen?"

"She says, 'sometimes you have to laugh' which I think is good advice for marriage and for life in general," noted Ellen.

We continued to play. Molly mentioned that she was going to catch a ride to Grand Rapids with the guys who were going to the hockey game because she had a flight out to Columbus that night. "Very convenient for you," observed Kat. "I think that Chuck is picking up one of those big vans from the dealership so there will be lots of room for everyone."

Molly responded, "It helps me out, it is just a quick trip and last minute. This worked out perfectly."

"Who is going to pick you up from the airport after your trip?" asked Ellen.

Molly seemed flustered, "I don't know, it's fine, it's covered."

"Are you planning on leaving your gloves in his truck again?" asked Ellen.

Molly nodded her head and stated, "Don't be silly."

CHAPTER 23

Lace-Up Boots

Despite her out-of-town trip, Molly was back and ready to play. The weather had taken a nasty turn, and it was very cold and blustery. Molly was wearing a beautiful coat and fashionable boots and looked stunning as she entered the coffee shop. I felt a little sloppy in my snow boots and puffy coat. For March it was quite frigid and fashion-wise I was doing the best I could.

The bakery did not disappoint with large samples of a crispy treat with sugar topping. It was just the thing to take one's mind off the crappy weather and disappointment that there would probably not be an early spring. As I went into the shop, I saw Lisa was also substituting that week.

She and Molly were chatting as we waited for the fourth player. The owner of the coffee shop stopped at the table and asked if Mrs. M. would be there today. I told her no and the owner told us, "When you talk to her can you mention that I need to touch base with her on the new Little League uniforms." We must have looked confused, she continued, "She has sponsored our team since her boys played, I thought you knew that." We nodded and the owner smiled and left the table.

Ellen came through the door with red cheeks and a warm looking hat. She also had her own Mah Jongg set with her. She sat down and explained, "Kat is working that strange split shift thing today, it is a good thing that you could get away Lisa."

Lisa nodded, "So Mrs. M. isn't going to be here today?"

"No, but Darcy is here so we are all set," noted Ellen. "Have you played this year Lisa? I can't remember the last time I saw you."

Lisa answered, "It has been a minute. I can usually get away if you need me. The girls had colds early in the year and of course, not at the same time. I was wiping little noses for about six straight weeks. They are just coming out of it now."

"My one son had a sinus infection," remarked Ellen. "He was just so dramatic, he remarked 'Just leave me here to die.' He was miserable but he got over it in about a week and no one else has been sick."

Lisa asked, "Where is that drama coming from?"

"I blame the teenage years," said Ellen. "I'm ready to march right over to the assisted living home and ask my mother-in-law what Dean was like at that age."

I nodded in agreement.

Lisa remarked, "I'm glad that mine are still little. They are so much fun. My husband and I are going to a conference, and they are going to spend a few days with Grandma next week."

"Mrs. M?" Molly asked.

Lisa responded, "No, my mom. They just love her

and that cat. My husband suggested my mom take them, just to spread a little grandma fun around as he told me."

In my mind I'm putting the pieces together, the fact that Mrs. M,'s son knows that she is sick, but Lisa does not, so he suggested Lisa's mom babysit. It made sense to me.

Ellen asked, "Where are you going?"

"Chicago, but it is just for three nights," stated Lisa. "I enjoy these little getaways, and my mom loves taking the girls. By the way, Ellen, I never heard anything from you about your brother-in-law. My cousin is still available."

Ellen noted, "He seems to be getting into the groove of living here. Right now, I would say his focus is my in-laws. They are out at the assisted living place, and he spends most of his free time with them. Thanks for reminding me though. By the way, what did Mrs. M. bring the girls from her trip to Wales?"

"Paddington bear backpacks," Lisa told them. "With a King Charles hankie in each one, she told me to be sure to mention that to you. Are hankies an inside joke?"

Ellen replied, "I wish. It would be less embarrassing. Somehow the whole King Charles thing got started and now it has snowballed out of control, and I can't stop it."

"I'm not sure I get it," commented Lisa. "Do you like King Charles?"

Ellen responded, "He is very nice, I'm sure. I just mentioned him one time and I have been haunted by him ever since."

"Mrs. M. has that sort of sense of humor," noted Lisa. "Unfortunately, you are most likely marked for life, I should know."

Ellen asked, "Does she tease you about something?"

"I don't want to talk about it," responded Lisa. "Needless to say, I will never be able to wear lace-up boots again."

Ellen noted, "Probably just as well."

CHAPTER 24

The Baby Picture Diversion

It was an April day that could have been mistaken for summer. I parked in the lot down the block and was practically skipping as I arrived at the coffee shop. The shop itself seemed festive in its own way and smelled heavily of sugar as I walked in. Directly to my right in the window was a very traditional looking wedding cake that I was sure was destined for an upcoming nuptial.

There were what I would call parts of tarts as samples at the front counter. All in all, it seemed like a very uplifting type of day. Sitting at the regular Mah Jongg table was Alexis. She was a beautiful woman who I knew for a fact was in her late 40's although I thought that she looked much younger.

The last time I saw her was before I joined the group and before she had her twins. I was calculating in my head that the babies were probably eight or nine months old by now.

I walked up to the table and introduced myself. I could tell by the look in her eye that she realized that every time she had substituted for Mah Jongg the previous year I was there. She didn't say anything, but I was sure that she knew. I told her that Kat had mentioned the twins, Josey and Jake and commented on and on how cute they are. Alexis laughed, "They do keep me hopping. I have to say they are good sleepers, those two. When I put them to bed, they entertain each other until one falls asleep. I have it on the baby cam."

"How old are they?" I asked.

Alexis stated, "Almost eleven months. Josey is walking, and Jake is right behind her on that milestone. I don't remember any of my other kids walking before they turned one year old, but I guess every baby is different. While I have you here, you were the one who gave Kat some ideas for her wedding, weren't you? I appreciate it. I think it is going to work out great."

"I'm not sure," I explained and laughed. "I don't want to be cornered in a dark alley by Rachel because I suggested matching dresses. I don't even know her, and I'm a little afraid of her."

"Do you have sisters?" asked Alexis. "There is a little bit of competition there, always has been. They do have each other's backs. By the way, I'm substituting for Mrs. M. today. Do you know where she is?"

I replied, "I have no idea. Maybe she went back to Europe." Of course, I knew full well that Mrs. M.'s lung cancer was removed, and she was out of the hospital, but I was sworn to secrecy.

"You said that with a straight face," Alexis observed. "My husband is a physician, and he won't tell me anything either."

I noted changing the subject, "I would love to see pictures of those twins."

Just then Ellen came into the coffee shop dressed in a very sharp lightweight sweater set which I had not seen before. It matched her eyes perfectly and I realized that I had never noticed how blue they were. It was a small detail that had not really caught my attention until today. Molly followed soon after and we all sat down to play.

Alexis asked, "Have you ladies started planning Kat's wedding shower yet or is she even having one? I am not asking so much for myself as my husband, Carl. Do you remember the last shower, with the axe throwing? He still talks about it. Heaven knows they will want to up their game the next time, I am thinking that there will be explosions involved. Regardless, it is April and the wedding is in June. Chop, chop!"

"We have some plans; you'll get an update soon. She may not want to have one. I mean they have everything they need between them. They aren't teenagers." Ellen explained. Then she added sarcastically, "It is going to be a great summer regardless, you know how much I look forward to baseball season." That comment produced laughter from Alexis.

As we played it was obvious that Alexis had not lost her touch. She won three games in a row. As we were setting up the walls for the next game Ellen's brother-in-law Bill came into the shop and to the table. I could see the resemblance to Ellen's husband Dean but he was not like I pictured him. He had a shy, awkward, hesitant look about him, but very kind eyes.

He greeted the group and said he was on his lunch break and indicated that he was looking for Kat.

When he saw that she was not there, he turned directly to Molly and asked "Are you going to see her? I took the drawers out of the vanity in her old apartment to fix a squeak and this necklace fell out. Do you know if it is hers? Mrs. Grebe didn't think she had ever seen it."

He put the necklace in Molly's hand, and she laughed nervously. It was a diamond solitaire on a nice chain and looked almost antique. Bill said "l didn't mean to put you on the spot; I thought Kat would be here. But I'm glad to see you." He looked around the table and remarked, "It is nice to see all of you ladies. Sorry for the interruption." He briefly touched Molly's shoulder as he left and said his good-byes. It reminded me of Chuck looking for Kat in the coffee shop last year. Was it an astounding coincidence or just the universe's way of seeing if we were paying attention?

Alexis apparently was unfazed and noted, "Your brother-in-law is so sweet, I didn't ever actually meet him before today. My husband, Carl had that broken tooth, and Bill was the dentist on call and did a great job. He is going to be a substitute on the golf league starting in May."

"Did you know he was a golfer, Molly?" asked Ellen. "You golf, don't you?"

Molly laughed, "I do golf, and you know that. You are about as subtle as a sledgehammer." She turned to Alexis, "Ellen is on a one-woman quest to make me into a double sister-in-law."

"Is it working?" asked Alexis.

Molly replied, "Let's see some pictures of those babies."

"You know Mrs. M. would insist on an answer," Alexis noted.

Molly laughed, "I guess I'm lucky she isn't here today then.

Everyone laughed and eventually we did get to see the photos of the babies. As soon as I could I texted Mrs. M. about the whole Bill and the necklace situation, and she replied with a smiley face. Good enough, I thought to myself.

CHAPTER 25

Slip In Shoes

I was substituting for Mrs. M. for the fifth consecutive week, but no one initially mentioned anything. I really didn't have any information to give even if they asked me. The new Mah Jongg cards had come out and there was a lengthy discussion about that. Spring was really blooming outside, and the ladies were all dressed for the weather.

"Any plans for Spring Break?" Ellen asked.

Kat lifted both arms up and exclaimed, "SPRING BREAK."

"It was kind of a rough winter for my mother-in-law," stated Ellen. "I'm glad that the weather is getting better. The place Dean's parents live is nice but there isn't as much green space as I would like. It is hard to bring her over to our house because of the whole wheelchair thing."

Molly asked, "How is she doing by the way?"

"You know she isn't really doing well," Ellen replied. "However, my father-in-law is in great shape. He keeps a car over there and still drives, but again, it is hard to get her in and out of the car to go anywhere. I think they would have kept the house if both were in as good physical shape as he is. I think seeing Bill more has made his mother happy so that is a plus."

Molly noted, "It seems like it would be a nice place. I think that you are right about the lack of green space."

"Yes, but there are quite a few positives to the place. For one, the young girls who work there are so sweet," Ellen responded. "There is one gal, Maria who has this really unique accent. I keep thinking that she is from Mexico but that isn't quite it. It is interesting to just listen to her voice. She seems to brighten up my mother-in-law's day when she is around."

Molly replied, "I think that she speaks Castilian Spanish. It is Spanish, just Spanish from Spain."

"How do you know her?" asked Ellen.

Molly replied, "I don't know, around, you know, yoga. I'm going up to get a cookie sample, anyone?"

I jumped in, "Did you hear that it is going to get down to 35 degrees this week? I have been very concerned with my rhubarb plants. Should I cover them if it gets colder?"

"I would," Kat volunteered. "Rhubarb is pretty hardy, but you never know, it can get really cold at night around this time of year. I wonder if Mrs. M. is busy putting in her garden, she can really get lost in it. I feel like we have not seen her for a long time."

Ellen commented, "Darcy, how many weeks have you subbed for Mrs. M. in a row?"

"Just a couple," I replied, knowing full well it had been five weeks but not wanting to let on to the others that it had been a long time.

Ellen noted, "It seems longer. Of course, this time of year when we're waiting for a Michigan summer, time does sort of drag. The boys are signed up for spring and summer baseball. They are on the same team, and it is exciting for them. My biggest issue with baseball is I can't for the life of me I can't figure out why they wear white uniforms, grass stains are hard to get out."

"Spoken like a true sports fan," noted Kat.

While they were discussing the ins and outs of youth sports, I let my mind wonder why Molly knew someone from the assisted living place where Ellen's in-laws lived. Had she visited over there with Bill? Were her parents living there? Did she have a secret life where she visited random elderly people? I wondered if I should report my findings to Mrs. M.

I decided that I definitely would.

The owner of the coffee shop stopped by the table with a free cookie for each of us. She wanted us to know that they would be closed for two weeks for renovation. She told us "I hope to see all of you in three weeks. And Kat we need to set up that cake tasting once we're up and running again."

As she walked away, Ellen laughed and remarked, "What a rarity, the words Kat and cake in the same sentence. Who would have thought?" Ellen continued. "So, Kat whatever happened with that necklace that Bill brought to Molly?"

Kat explained, "I had never seen it before, it may have been from a previous tenant. The fact that Mrs. Grebe didn't recognize it means it is really old."

"Where did you leave it?" asked Ellen.

Kat laughed, "Right where Bill put it, in Molly's

hand. He didn't want it back."

"What are you going to do with it, Molly?" Ellen inquired.

Molly replied, "Not sure, it is like something I didn't know I wanted until I got it."

"That is exactly how I feel about my slip in shoes." Ellen stated. "They changed my life."

Kat laughed, "You are such a mom, if Mrs. M. was here, it would be the King Charles thing all over again."

"Oh yes, it would. I would never live down the fact that I love my slip in shoes, it is a hill that I am willing to die on," agreed Ellen. "I don't care, as I told all of you, they changed my life."

There were giggles all around and game went on.

CHAPTER 26

The Secret Sister-In-Law Society

The weather was balmy for May in Northern Michigan. Three weeks had passed, and the renovations at the coffee shop were complete although I must admit I didn't see very much change. I was substituting for Molly and Mrs. M. was back. She had been gone for at least two months.

I was already seated and as she passed by me, she softly squeezed my shoulder. At first glance, she looked exactly the same. She was dressed in a light-weight sweater and matching skirt and was wearing matching flats. I wondered what kind of treatment she was on after her lung cancer surgery since she hadn't lost her hair. She did look a bit tired, especially around her eyes.

Ellen and Kat came in and the game was set up quickly. Kat asked Ellen how her mother-in-law was doing. "Not well," stated Ellen. "I was over there yesterday, and she seemed frail. She is in her 70s so I'm not surprised. I was thinking back many years ago when I first met her, and she seemed so active then."

Mrs. M. interjected, "Well you know, we all get there."

"I know," noted Ellen. "It is just I remember every time Dean and I went over to their house, they lived in Buckley at that time, when we were dating, and we would play outdoor games. They liked croquette and bocce balls, and we always played boys against girls. Dean's mom and I would absolutely demolish the boys. She was a force to be reckoned with back then. By the way Kat, do you know who stopped by and left her and my father-in-law that sample box of small cakes?"

Kat answered laughing, "Can't say that I do but it sounds like a fab thing. I have to say that I'm a little offended that you would think something involving cake came from me."

"Very funny. I'm glad that you are here today, Mrs. M.," observed Ellen changing the topic. "We have had the hardest time getting any information out of the secret sisters-in-law club members here. By we, I mean me because you know I always want to know everything."

Mrs. M. asked, "What has been going on with Molly? I haven't seen her in the longest time."

"She is good," replied Kat. "She met me for a walk recently and we had a chance to talk. Now I think you missed this part Mrs. M., but Bill found a necklace in my old apartment. He brought the necklace to Mah Jongg, thinking I would be there that day. Since I wasn't there, he gave it to Molly, and she brought it to me."

Mrs. M. noted as she slyly looked over at me, "Wow, was it yours?"

"No," Kat replied. "It didn't belong to Mrs. Grebe either, so it is a mystery. It is really a nice diamond necklace, an antique obviously, but worth a couple of grand. The diamond is huge and very good quality for a necklace; it is big enough for a nice ring."

"Is he going to sell it?" asked Mrs. M.

Kat laughed, "No, he gave it to Molly. She told me that he told her 'I wouldn't have put it in your hand if I didn't want you to have it' or something like that."

"I have only one thing to say, sappy," remarked Ellen. "Something is going on there, I'm beginning to put the pieces together on this and I will."

Kat replied, "She hasn't let anything slip, but now that the great interrogator is back with us, we may be able to get to the bottom of this."

"Speaking of the bottom, how are things at the bottom of the barrel, Ellen?" asked Mrs. M. coughing. "Have you conducted any bilingual workshops lately?"

Ellen replied, "Don't be so quick to assume I'm at the bottom of the barrel. I just gave a wonderful workshop called 'You and the Interview' and over half of the participants spoke English. I considered it a success."

"Are you working much over the summer?" asked Kat.

"I doubt it, the schedule is lighter over there and of course am going to be busy toting the boys back and forth to baseball," stated Ellen. "Their team is sponsored by the towing company, which is a step up from last year when it was sponsored by the trash hauler."

Kat laughed, "I loved the uniforms last year with the trash truck on them. Speaking of which, I wonder what the coffee shop team uniforms will look like this year?" She turned to Mrs. M. and asked, "Do you know? You should since you bought them for the team."

Mrs. M. stopped playing for a moment, coughed and stated, "It's nothing, not worth mentioning. The uniforms are very small. It's T-ball for goodness's sake."

CHAPTER 27

Field Day goes Awry

The weather had been beautiful for over a week and that day was no exception. Before leaving for Mah Jongg, I had washed my winter puffy coat and put all of my sweaters and winter clothing away. Mrs. M. asked me to substitute for her due to an urgent medical appointment, she seemed to be coughing frequently so naturally I was concerned.

Kat and Molly walked in together and neither were wearing coats. Kat seemed very relaxed for someone who was getting married within a few weeks and she and Molly gave me a big wave as they entered the coffee shop. Both stopped at the front counter to grab a sample and then plopped down at the table. Kat noted excitedly, "I can't wait to see Ellen. Apparently, Field Day at the school was quite a thing."

"What happened, was it the riot that she expected?" I inquired. Just then Ellen walked in and sat down.

We set up the game and Kat asked about Field Day. Ellen laughed and told us "First, let me say Annie's teacher Mrs. Rinaldi should be in charge of the whole thing. Her class was right on point."

I asked, "I know the concept but what do they actually do?"

"They have games," stated Ellen. "It is one class

against the other or boys against the girls or any combination. Some of the other teachers apparently did not get the memo and were walking the field in high heels and skirts. Of course, when you let two hundred kids outside at the same time chaos ensues. It was like tornados of little people swirling around everywhere."

"Were the other parents helping?" Molly asked.

Ellen laughed, "Reverend Bob was there. He was helping one of the other teachers since Mrs. Rinaldi and I had Annie's class under control. At one point he was trying to stop someone from running wild and he put his arm out like the safety patrol and this kid ran right into his arm and flipped completely over and landed on her feet. It was quite a thing."

I noted, "I bet that was funny."

"Oh yes," Ellen responded. "Once the gym teacher started using the whistle things calmed down. They did the tug of war and that was popular, the class in each division who won got a pizza day in the future and a little trophy to keep in their room. They did races, starting with large groups and ending up with one winner. That person got a prize. The last game had all the teachers kicking a ball. Whoever kicked the furthest won cookies for their class. The pressure was really on for the teachers. Well, that was hysterical because two of the teachers were kicking in heels. They both kicked their shoes clean off, and their shoes went flying down the field, unlike the kickball. Fun to watch."

Molly asked, "Who won?"

"Mrs. Rinaldi, of course," Ellen replied. "That woman is a force of nature."

CHAPTER 28

Oh, THAT Judge

I haven't substituted in a few weeks, and the weather was just exactly what one would expect for a June day. The flowers were out and so were the teenagers. I was aware that Kat was getting married on Friday and leaving for her honeymoon on Saturday, so I assumed I was subbing for her. I was surprised to see her walk in.

Kat stopped to pick up a cake sample and walked over to the table, before she sat down, she gave me a little side hug. She remarked, "Thank you again for setting me up with your sister to officiate the wedding.I didn't realize that she was THAT judge. You never told us anything."

"I only see my sister as the person who cut my hair when I was four and I was the one who got in trouble for it. Even back then she could argue a case. How is all the rest of the planning going?" I asked.

Kat noted "It is all working out really well. I mean we're only having 10 people in total besides us, your sister and a photographer. You should see the dresses for the girls. They are totally cute and even Rachel had to say that she liked them."

"Fab," I stated. "I wanted to mention to you that since you will have photos from the wedding you could put them on the invitation for the party you are having in August. We did something like that. It is just an idea."

Kat replied excitedly, "Oh my gosh, another great idea. We are so going to do that. Chuck will love that. I feel a little bad that you and Mrs. M. won't be at the wedding. It is very small and if we invited Uncle Stan, we would have to invite Chuck's mom and my dad's other siblings and their partners, and it would just get big."

"Understood," I commented. "So that Uncle Stan thing is still percolating along?"

Kat noted, "I wish I knew, between Mrs. M. and Molly it is like everyone is so evasive about their personal lives, which I respect. Also, I meant to ask you. Did it seem like Mrs. M. was gone for a long time around Easter? I was looking at her when we were playing the other day and she looked a little tired around the eyes. Did you notice that?"

"Maybe," I noted. "She always looks so nice. I'm usually focused on her tasteful and seasonally appropriate outfits."

Just then Ellen and Molly came in and started walking towards the table. They sat down and we started playing with a new Mah Jongg set that Molly had brought with her. I commented on how nice it was, and she told us that it was a gift since she was a whole year cancer free.

I said, "I'm so glad to hear that, you must be thrilled."

"I can't believe that I have been playing all these

years and never had a set," noted Molly.

We continued to play and during a break, I texted Mrs. M. that Molly had a new Mah Jongg set. She texted me back, 'Find out if it was from Bill, use pressure or trickery if necessary.'

That made me laugh and when we all got back to the table it was Ellen who asked where the Mah Jongg set was purchased. Molly replied, "I don't know, it was a gift."

I remarked, "I know that they have that big game shop in Grand Rapids, I wonder if it was purchased there. It isn't an item that you can buy locally. Of course he could have bought it online."

Molly blushed a little, laughed and stated, "It is as if you are channeling Mrs. M. there Darcy. By the way, where IS Mrs. M?"

"Well, based on Darcy's questioning Mrs. M. is at least here in spirit," Ellen declared laughing. "You should know Darcy that I'm related to Bill, and I get nothing from him about whether something is or is not going on. The only clue that I have is that my husband asked me where to buy a Mah Jongg set. I think that is a pretty big clue."

Molly laughed, "You know that inquiry could be for anyone, maybe someone at his Machine Shop wants to learn to play Mah Jongg. Machinists are known for their love of Mah Jongg."

"Likely untrue, but funny nonetheless," Ellen said, and the play continued.

CHAPTER 29

A Swing and A Miss

I was expecting an exciting recap of Kat's wedding, so I was anxious to get to Mah Jongg and get the full scoop. Alexis was already there with her babies and their nanny. The babies were sleeping in their double stroller despite the noise of the coffee shop. They were very cute just as advertised.

Alexis greeted me and told me immediately, "I met your sister at the wedding. Now that I have seen you again, I can see the resemblance. She did a great job officiating. I think that Chuck was more nervous than Kat. He gave her the longest kiss at the end. Luckily it was just family there."

"I haven't spoken to my sister, so thanks for the update," I noted. "I bet that everyone looked great. I can't wait to see the photos."

Alexis continued, "You know my husband and I sort of stood in for Kat's parents. They passed away many years ago. Did she tell you that she had wedding leis made for the occasion? I can't remember the last time I wore one of those. I thought that the whole thing was perfect."

"And they are off on their honeymoon to Hawaii now?" I asked.

Alexis asked, "Where else? We were reminiscing

about our honeymoon after the ceremony. You know my husband and I had no money when we got married, he had just finished medical school, and I was working two jobs. We went to a cottage my uncle had on the Manistee River. We didn't realize that there was heavy canoe traffic on the river. So, on the first day that we were there we came walking out to do some nude sunbathing and all of a sudden there were like seven canoes full of Boy Scouts paddling down the river."

"I bet that was a shock," I stated.

Alexis laughed, "For everyone involved. Doesn't it seem like everyone has a funny story from their honeymoon? You never hear someone say, 'Nothing happened.' There is always a story."

"Speaking of stories, did Molly have a good time at the wedding?" I asked Alexis.

Alexis noted, "Yes, I believe everyone had a good time. I hadn't had an opportunity to talk to Ellen's brother-in-law, Bill prior to the wedding, and he seemed really nice but very shy. I have heard that he is an excellent dentist. I may be looking to switch. Dr. Brouwer is retiring soon. Anyway, getting back to this Bill guy, I think that he and Molly were the only single people there, they seemed to know each other somewhat. I think she is seeing a firefighter, right?"

"Word is, that ended last fall," I explained.

Alexis laughed, "You miss a lot when you have two newborns. I honestly don't remember much that happened between June and let's say March of this year. I think that I'm finally out of the baby fog. The funny part is that they were good sleepers right from the get-go. I was the one who didn't sleep great. My husband on the other hand, has always been able to sleep through anything."

"I can relate," I mused.

Mrs. M. and Ellen entered the shop and the moment they saw the stroller; both made a beeline for the table. Mrs. M. observed, "I finally get to see these little Havens. They are so darling."

Alexis noted, "They seem to be sleeping through their debut. The nanny can take them for a walk and when they wake up, she can come back. Does that work for you guys?"

"Sure," answered Ellen. "It is the eleventh commandment, never wake a sleeping baby."

The nanny and babies left, and we set up the game and started playing. Mrs. M. stated, "You know Alexis, I can't remember when the last time was, I saw you."

Alexis answered, "It has been a minute, how is the summer going?'

"Good," Mrs. M. noted as she coughed. "But my garden is a disappointment."

Ellen asked, "How is your T-ball team doing, Mrs. M.?"

"According to the coach, they are not wandering around the field like they did the first few weeks," remarked Mrs. M. She turned to Alexis, "Ellen is teasing me all the time because I paid for the uniforms for the T-ball team that the coffee shop sponsors. She called me Steinbratter the other day."

Alexis laughed, "I think that she meant Steinbrenner."

"There you go, Ellen," stated Mrs. M. "A swing and a miss."

CHAPTER 30

Not a Felon

I was not surprised that I was asked to substitute this week, due to the fact that I knew that Kat was still on her honeymoon. The weather felt almost like Hawaii. Mrs. M. was already seated when I arrived, and she had a troubled look on her face until she saw me and then she smiled.

She told me, "I appreciate it that you were able to keep my surgery to yourself. I don't know if I told you, but my sister Martha died of lung cancer, and she wasn't a smoker either. I just couldn't tell people who were around when I lost her. I was afraid I would get too emotional."

"Completely understood," I told her. "I'm still carrying around some secrets from my college days, I'm a vault. Otherwise, how do you feel now?"

Mrs. M. sighed and explained, "Not great. I just have to do what they tell me to do and keep moving ahead with my life. Stan has been a big help. I know people wonder about us and it tickles me to keep that a bit of a mystery."

"It especially drives Ellen crazy," I noted.

Mrs. M. coughed and laughed, "She has always been one of those people who has to know everything. Strangely enough she has not been able to put together the Bill and Molly situation. I knew that was in play from the day she left her gloves in his truck."

"In terms of Ellen, you know her mother-in-law hasn't been well," I volunteered. "I think that situation takes up a lot of her emotional bandwidth. I do think that Molly may have dropped those cake samples off at the assisted living place which means she probably went with Bill. Plus, she knew that one worker was from Spain. There are several clues here, but you never know if anything will come of it."

Mrs. M. observed, "True. They don't have to get serious. We may be jumping the gun."

Just then Ellen came in, breathless. She told us, "Get this one, look at this picture from the wedding. Molly is wearing that necklace."

Mrs. M. laughed, "Are you planning on interrogating her about it?"

"That is your job, Mrs. M., you are good at it," Ellen replied.

Mrs. M. asked, "What transpired at the wedding? Was there any telling, interaction there?"

"There was a lot going on overall. I didn't see much that was obvious couple stuff between Bill and Molly. They seemed cordial. You know speaking of the wedding," noted Ellen. "One of the nicest parts was when my dad welcomed Kat to the family. Everyone was emotional at that point. He talked about Rachel and me and how great we were and then he said, 'I didn't think that there were any more perfect daughters in the world than Rachel and Ellen until I met Kat. I know now that there is one more.' It was just a lot for our dad to say that. He is generally a man of few words."

I told them, "That is so sweet, it sounds like it was right from the heart. Of course, the big question is, how was the cake?"

"Cakes. She had three cakes, and they were just fabulous," Ellen noted. Just then Molly walked in. Ellen directed her question to Molly, "What did you think of the cakes at the wedding, which one would you choose if you were getting married?"

Molly laughed, "You aren't nearly as good at subtle interrogation as Mrs. M., you better step up your game!"

"Which one was the best?" asked Ellen.

Molly replied, "I did like the coconut cake the best. It is not often you have three cakes to choose from."

"Or have over twenty-five percent of the people there dressed as bridesmaids. You don't see that often either," observed Ellen. "I met the photographer at the door, and he was very confused. He asked me if the audience would be standing during the ceremony, and I told him there were only four people there who were not in the wedding. Luckily the judge was clued in by Darcy, so she knew what to expect."

I asked, "Can I see the photos? Is there one with my sister in it?"

"Yes, I have a few on my phone. Kat will probably bring in the whole album once she gets back. As for your sister, she really is a lot taller than you, isn't she?" asked Ellen. "While we were having cake, she had some very funny stories about marriages that she had officiated. Did she ever tell you about the guy she sentenced to nine months in jail and officiated his wedding the same day? She told me that the sentence lasted longer than the marriage. Of course, Kat and Chuck are solid."

I noted, "Well neither is a felon, they have that going for them."

CHAPTER 31

SWAT Team Maneuvers

Kat was still away, and Alexis stepped in but did not bring her babies. It was nice to see her anyway. Before we could start talking, Ellen and Molly walked into the coffee shop together. It was a rainy, oppressively hot day, by Northern Michigan standards. Sort of a humid fog hung over the town, and it was just wet feeling outside. To be honest, everyone in the group looked a little wilted.

As we set up the game and started playing, Alexis asked Ellen how baseball was going for her boys. Ellen laughed and noted that she had to buy a giant hat to wear to the games. Ellen said, "It is either hot, hot, hot or a rainout. There are times I almost root for a rainout. I thank my lucky stars that the boys are both on the same team."

I asked, "How are they doing?"

"Just well enough that they will probably go on to the next step, semis of whatever, but not good enough to win anything big," Ellen responded. "I wish that they were either a little better or a little worse. My mom and dad were at the game yesterday and both boys were waving and yelling 'Hey grandpa' to my dad. I say, no love for your own mother or even my mother?"

Alexis told us, "That is so funny. Since I have raised both boys and girls, I can tell you they both continue to be a mystery to me. The other day the babies were doing some sort of thing where they would come around the side of the couch and startle each other. Jake fell for it every time. Josey, not so much."

"I bet they are fun to watch," I noted.

Alexis laughed, "You have no idea. The other day, and keep in mind that these little ones are only 13 months old, they were doing this whole SWAT team maneuver. They were looking for something silently pointing at things and pointing at their eyes like they were ready to storm a drug house. I almost got out my phone to film it, but I just wanted to sit there and enjoy it."

Ellen remarked, "You have to wonder what they were looking for."

"That thought did cross my mind, whatever it was, I don't think that they located it," noted Alexis. "They really don't talk well enough to get any help from me on that one. They can put together a sentence now and then which seems advanced, but I'm biased on that count."

Molly laughed and commented, "They are probably plotting to take over the house."

"They do chat with each other in their cribs at night," Alexis explained. "My husband Carl went to check on them one night. They were standing up in their cribs talking and he swears one shushed the other and they stopped talking when he walked in. I didn't have the monitor on, but I would not doubt it.

Since this is my third set of twins, I know the power of two little people is a force to be reckoned with."

Ellen stated, "Talk about a force to be reckoned with, you have two teenage girls. I would be more concerned about that dynamic."

"That is working to my advantage right now," Alexis continued. "Apparently some cute guys from their school are helping out at the baby swim classes this summer. Once they found that out, they volunteered to take the babies. Of course, they needed two new swimsuits each in order to participate. The giggling is out of control. I love it, I just sit and watch by the side of the pool drinking an iced tea, two weeks to go."

Ellen asked, "They drive, right?"

"They are sharing a car," answered Alexis. "I would rather they don't drive the babies though. That is fine with them, I think they are hoping to go out after class with one of those cute boys from the swim class. Babies can really intrude on your social calendar."

Molly asked, "Do you ever think about the fact that fifteen years from now the babies will be driving?"

"Right now, I'm just trying to figure out what to do once the babies figure out how to get out of the playpen," answered Alexis. "They were sizing it up the other day, I think they are planning an escape."

Molly laughed, "If they show up at my place I will give you a call."

CHAPTER 32

Surf Lessons

You can't beat a Michigan summer. That is what I was thinking to myself as I walked down the street towards the coffee shop. There was not a cloud in the sky and the breeze was warm. It reminded me of my summers on Mill Lake and all the fun we had jumping off the dock and swimming out to the stationary pier that our neighbors had anchored several yards offshore. Today, however, I was headed for my Mah Jongg game and looking forward to catching up with everyone there.

This was a busy summer for all the players except me. Kat got married in June and was planning her reception in August. My sister had performed the ceremony, and we had recently had coffee together, so I was able to get her impressions of all the various players. In terms of Kat and Chuck, my sister said that they looked like two people who were somehow destined to be together and seemed to be having a lot of fun. I asked about Molly and Bill, but she did not seem to remember them well. I admonished her because there were only like twelve people there. My sister noted, "Yes, twelve people that I didn't know."

I had to agree with her on that one. She indicated that Kat and Chuck tried to pay her for her services, but she politely declined. She did, however, take a couple of pieces of cake home and told me that they were fabulous.

I walked into the coffee shop and picked up a very crispy apple item that smelled like cinnamon heaven. I sat down with a cup of tea and waited for the others to arrive. I had not seen Kat since she returned from her honeymoon. When she walked in, I greeted her and I congratulated her on her marriage. She was in very good spirits and asked how I had been. Kat noted, "I'm finally back in the groove for work, I was off for more than two weeks and it seems like months. We just had fun every day on our honeymoon and even getting there and back was fine."

"What was the most fun you had?" I asked.

Kat laughed, "One place that we stayed was near where a river comes into the ocean on Kauai. Do you know it?"

"Near Lydgate Park?" I asked.

Kat continued, "Exactly. So, there were these people there taking surfing lessons. I guess the way the waves come in and those sandbars make it ideal for that. So, we sat there watching and at the same time trying to open a coconut with rocks. We were laughing so hard; it was just the best."

"Did you get over to the Big Island to see your peeps there?" I asked.

Kat laughed, "Oh yes, that was indeed a riot. We went down to the Volcano Park and all over the place. Of course, we had to hit the southernmost bakery in the United States in Naalehu. Needless to say, I sent

Ellen a postcard from there."

"I bet it was fun," I told her.

Kat continued, "They threw a little party for me right there in Pepeekeo. It reminded me too much of earlier times in my life. I just had to stand on the cliff and take it all in. It almost seems like some sort of a doorway to me. I stand on the edge of the island, the edge of the country and the edge of the ocean. I have come a long way from that time in my life. It is good to remember."

"Sometimes I get taken in by the moment," I mused. "When I go to warm weather places it takes me right back to a specific time in my life. I don't exactly miss it, but I just feel the way I felt then for a moment."

Kat asked, "I get that. I have a very specific reaction when I'm flying above any landscape where the ocean meets the shore. I can't describe it. It is sort of a metaphysical moment. It makes me think about what is real and how differently we see things from different places. I find it peaceful and scary at the same time."

"I can see that, I wonder about the ocean and how long it has been there and how it is always the same and always different," I observed.

Kat smiled, "Well I guess we delved deep into things there. What did I miss here?"

"Well, Alexis subbed one day," I remarked. "She had us laughing really hard with stories about the babies. Ask her about the SWAT team story and the swimming lessons, you will laugh over those two. In other news, Ellen's mother-in-law is still not well and Ellen is deeply involved in youth baseball right now. You should know that the cakes at your wedding were very positively reviewed."

Kat inquired, "Molly and Bill?"

"Still a summer mystery or perhaps a summer romance," I noted.

Molly herself and Ellen arrived just at that moment. They were happy to see Kat as well and congratulated her. Ellen asked, "Did Darcy fill you in on all you missed? You know I loved the postcard from the bakery. Was that an all-day excursion?"

Kat laughed, "Very funny. We did have fun though and we were thinking of you guys and how nice you made the wedding. Chuck and I talked about it every day. He kept saying we should just stay there and never come back. Wishful thinking."

We started setting up the tiles and Kat noted excitedly, "This is my first Mah Jongg game as a married woman."

"Aww," I noted.

"Sappy," Ellen replied.

CHAPTER 33

Listen Up

It had been a few weeks since I played. Summer was winding down. As soon as I walked into the coffee shop, I knew something was off. Kat was sitting alone at the Mah Jongg table, and she softly motioned for me to come over and she looked like she had been crying. I sat down and prepared myself for something bad.

"Mrs. M. is in the hospital," Kat told me. "She has been sick for a long time. I wouldn't even have known but I just happened to see Uncle Stan come in when I was coming off of my shift yesterday. He told me that she had been sick for more than two months. She never said anything to anyone. I'm at a loss."

I responded, "I think it is natural to feel that way. Do you feel that you could go see her in the hospital? That would put your mind at ease a little maybe."

"She has lung cancer," Kat stated, her voice breaking. "I wish now I had asked her to be at the wedding. You know her sister died of lung cancer. She could die."

I scootched my chair over a little and put an arm around Kat. "You know that she is a private person, she probably didn't want to worry anyone. She is also a strong person; she may pull out of this. What do you actually know?"

Kat told us, "She is in the hospital because of some secondary infection which is rare this long after surgery. The surgery was over two months ago. I wish that I had known. I was just rolling along with my life, I didn't even know."

Ellen and Molly came in and walked directly over to the table. Ellen looked at me and asked, "Did Kat fill you in?"

I nodded yes. Kat asked, "Do you think that Lisa knows? Since it is getting out there, I think someone should tell her."

I noted, "I'm sure she knows, her husband knew." I immediately realized that I had given my position away, but they did not seem to pick up on it.

Ellen asked, "Do you think that Uncle Stan told her that we all know? He was probably sworn to secrecy too."

"Would he say anything?" asked Kat. "Would he tell her that we know?"

In an epic moment of inner strength, Ellen straightened in her chair and stated, "Listen up. This is what we're going to do. We're going to pull ourselves together, we are going to call her and all talk to her and then we are going to play Mah Jongg." She picked up her phone and started the call. I heard Mrs. M. pick up the phone.

Kat was the last of us to speak to Mrs. M., although her hands and her voice were shaking, she held it together and promised to stop by before her shift that day.

Once Kat ended the call we started to play and talked sporadically about Mrs. M. Everyone seemed more at ease and Molly sat quietly tapping her foot under the table to the music coming from the speakers. What I first thought was sadness in her eyes was probably fear.

As we packed up to leave, Kat turned to Ellen and said, "I can't lose her."

Ellen pulled her closer and told her, "I know."

CHAPTER 34

Kale, No

It was a beautiful Michigan day. Mrs. M. had texted me to say she was home but wasn't feeling up to playing. Everyone came in looking strong and there was general discussion concerning Mrs. M.

Molly seemed to be especially cheery and at two different times she checked her phone and smiled to herself. Ellen noticed and asked her what was up. Molly replied "Joke of the day text." Ellen was skeptical but let it go.

Ellen asked, "How is married life, Kat?"

"Fun, fun, fun. I'm assuming all of you are coming to the luau/reception this weekend?" asked Kat.

Everyone nodded. Molly asked, "How many people are you expecting?"

"We have about fifty people coming," Kat replied. "Mrs. M. is definitely coming; I really want to see her. Some of my coworkers are coming too. Darcy, your sister, told me that she was out of town, but the photographer will be there to take casual photos. I guess that I am one of those people who always wants photos of everything."

Molly laughed, "What is the cake situation?"

"Over the top," noted Kat. "I'm giving prepackaged little cake boxes for everyone who wants one, plus the cakes themselves so, yes, I would say it is a cake overload. The whole thing is catered; I absolutely refuse to let my mother-in-law lift a finger on this one. She was teasing me when I told her that. I think that I may have inadvertently stomped my foot when I was expressing my thoughts on the situation."

Molly chimed in, "I'm trying to picture you stomping your little feet, trying to get your way. That is quite a picture."

"My new in-laws have done too much already," stated Kat. "I just want them to enjoy the party and have a good time. Speaking of which when the caterer came over, she brought her assistant, Sunshine, who I think babysits for Alexis sometimes. This girl is really sort of an earth mother type. She was telling me that she is teaching Jake and Josey sign language and apparently feeding them kale. Ick."

Ellen piped up, "Now it is all making sense, according to Alexis the babies are communicating up a storm with each other. She cracked me up with that whole SWAT team scenario she told us about."

"According to this babysitter," noted Kat, "These little ones are learning new words every day and new signs. That is so cool, I told Alexis to bring them to the luau. They can go in the shallow end of the pool with supervision, or I could get a kiddie pool just for that day."

Ellen asked, "Are you wearing the dress you wore to the wedding, Kat?"

"I'm sort of on the fence about that." Kat replied, "I mean it is fairly casual, but I think I will just wear the one that I bought that matches all of your dresses.

Ellen laughed, "I'm so, so, so looking forward to seeing Rachel in that dress again. I can't believe that you had one made for my little girl Annie. You know she showed it off to Rachel the other day and Rachel told her, 'You can have mine to wear when you get older.' I didn't know if that was sweet or a subtle dig at the dress because she just doesn't like being told what to wear or do."

"I love that dress," Molly noted. "I wore it to another get-together I went to, and I got lots of compliments. We should get some photos of all of us girls with the dresses on."

Ellen laughed, "You should be the one to bring that up to Rachel, or better yet I will send my little girl Annie in on that one. I can just hear her now, 'Oh Auntie Rachel, can they take a picture with all of us and our pretty dresses?' Rachel will not be able to say no to that."

"So, we are sending in seven-year-olds to do our dirty work now?" Molly asked.

Ellen replied, "Oh yes, we are."

CHAPTER 35

Trail of Cake

I was rushing back from Manistee and was the last one to arrive. Kat, Molly and Ellen had the game all set up. I sat down and listened to them discuss the recent luau party that Kat and Chuck had hosted to celebrate their recent wedding. Since I attended, I was wondering what other people thought about it.

Kat told us, "We ended up having about fifty people at the party. It was a good thing that we had three cakes. We have the top from the actual wedding day cake in the freezer and now we will have a second topper for later."

"Of course, because everyone was there for the cakes," Ellen responded. "I personally had a good time just putting my feet in the pool with a Mai Tai in my hand. Did that photographer take a lot of candid shots besides the ones that were posed?"

Kat answered, "Yes, he did and from what I can see they are good. Just as you predicted Annie asked Rachel to be in a photo in her dress and of course she had to comply. I was surprised that Rachel didn't immediately change after that, but she hung in there, Hawaiian dress and all."

"I thought everyone looked good," Molly noted. "It was also nice that so many people wore tropical shirts and the like. The flowers were wonderful too. It was nice of you to give some of the floral arrangements to Bill to take to the assisted living place."

Kat sighed, "I love flowers, but we bought six arrangements for the party and that is just too many to have around the house, I took one to work, and so did Rachel. Was Bill's mom happy with the flowers that you took over there Molly?"

"Yes, she was as a matter of fact," Molly replied. "And yes, I did go over there with Bill because there were so many flowers and little boxes of cake, he needed help bringing them all in. Also, his mom and dad loved the cake. How is your mother-in-law doing, Ellen? She seemed a little confused when we were there. For a minute, she thought that I was you."

Ellen noted, "She does seem to be having a hard time, I know they took her to the ER last week because she was having trouble breathing. She also had that same confusion with our boys and her sons, just for a moment she didn't seem to know who was who but then she got back on track."

"That is to be expected," Molly replied. "Interestingly your father-in-law was sharp as a tack. He was talking with Bill about how the Detroit Tigers are doing and was up on all the stats. He really dotes on your mother-in-law; she is a lucky woman."

Ellen replied, "They have always had a good marriage, and she has always been extremely sweet to me. My father-in-law doesn't really need any help with everyday life, so his only job is looking after her. Speaking of close oversight did you see Alexis and

Carl's babies?"

"I got a good close-up look at them," I stated. "They are so active, I don't know how she keeps up with them."

Molly chimed in, "I helped her take them in the pool. If you tell them to close their eyes and hold their breath they will, and you can just dip them underwater. They are going to be good swimmers. She is right about them; they have this whole communication system down. They are going to be a real handful down the line."

"That is true," Ellen noted. "I thought that the party was nice." Then she sarcastically added, "There were a few people at the party that I didn't know but you know how much I love to meet new people."

"Quite a few people from my work came," noted Kat. "There weren't many from Chuck's work who were invited since he is the big boss. Also, Stan and Mrs. M. were there. They seemed to be having a good time. He really caters to her, she was mostly just sitting there, and he was bringing her things."

Ellen stated, "You know my mom's other brothers were there too. They look just like Uncle Stan except they are both bald and heavy-set. Did you notice them?"

"Were they the two guys who were both wearing giant Hawaiian shirts and drinking beer?" asked Molly. "They seemed to be having a good time. I did see them, and I did think that they looked like someone I knew but I didn't put two and two together. I wasn't introduced."

Ellen laughed, "Probably a good thing, both will talk your ear off. They have the nicest wives, but these two guys just tell story after story after story about growing up and traveling. The poor women can't get a word in. You do not want to ask these guys about the Galapagos Islands, or you will be there for an hour."

"Well, someone's slides of Italy were what got this whole marriage thing started," noted Molly. "Although I think that Chuck might have found another way to get to Kat."

Ellen laughed, "Yes, all he would have had to do is just leave a trail of cake and Kat would have followed it straight back to him."

CHAPTER 36

Divots and Wine Coolers

I was the first person to arrive for Mah Jongg. Although the weather for Kat's luau was perfect it took a turn in the two and a half weeks since the event. It was only the second week of September, but it seemed chilly. I hadn't seen Mrs. M. since I spoke with her briefly at the event.

She came in shortly after I arrived and sat down immediately letting out a large sigh and coughed. She asked, "So what do you think about Bill and Molly?"

I replied, "Oh I think that they are more than friends, but I'm just not sure that is the biggest issue facing you right now."

"I know," Mrs. M. remarked. "You know my daughter-in-law is mad at me for not telling her that I was sick. I tried to explain but she felt left out, which I totally understand. I just want to move forward from here."

I asked, "How did you leave it with her?"

"She told me that she understood," Mrs. M. noted. "I could see in her eyes that she was hurt. You know I always try to handle things my own way and this time; I may have misjudged things."

I replied, "As an outsider, I think that you have to think of yourself first. You are in a fight for your survival, if there are hurt feelings along the way, so be it."

"That is basically what Rachel told me," Mrs. M. replied. "I talked to her at the luau, and she had cancer in the past. She understands. I have tried to explain that for my own sanity, I had to keep the circle small, or I might have fallen apart from all the talking about it."

I asked, "What are the doctors saying? If you don't mind me asking."

"It is about 50/50 that I will be in total remission in the next few months, or it could go the other way," Mrs. M. continued. "That infection set me back and I'm not a young woman anymore. Stan thinks that we should get married and travel as much as we can as long as I'm feeling able to. We had this deep heart-to-heart about whether his wanting to marry me is based on the cancer."

I asked, "What did he say?"

"He told me, 'The moment I saw you I just prayed that you wanted to come over and see my slides of Italy' and he laughed," Mrs. M. stated. "He lost his first wife, he knows what he is in for, still I believe the cancer doesn't matter to him. If anything, it makes him a better partner for me."

I sighed, "Aww, if Ellen was here, she would give that a sappy designation. That being said, you are within your rights to keep your private life private."

"Good advice," Mrs. M. responded. "I want to leave it like this. As far as you know, if you are asked, I'm doing much better. For all practical purposes I'm fully recovered, and Stan and I are just good friends. I know that you can keep up that facade for me."

I replied, "Of course, and you know that if you go on a trip, I will be texting you about the Bill and Molly situation as it develops. You know they have known each other for almost a year, and I still can't tell you where it is headed."

"I wasn't sure about him," noted Mrs. M. "He seemed like one of those guys who seemed to have very little personality. But at the luau, he was so funny. He was standing around with the guys telling stories about treating the hockey players and everyone was enjoying it. He glanced over at Molly at one point and gave her this little wave. She touched the necklace he gave her and smiled back. I guess you don't need fireworks every moment of every day to be a good match."

I laughed, "Sometimes less drama is better. In my marriage my husband and I have had a smooth ride, if it is hard work, we aren't doing any."

Ellen and Kat walked into the coffee shop and sat down at the table. Ellen asked lightly, "Are you ready to hear all of my complaints about Little League?"

"Love to," replied Mrs. M. It was as if nothing had transpired, and we were right where we had been a few months before. Everyone was able to pick up and move forward. Mrs. M. continued, "Is this about the batting order again or are we circling back to getting stains out of the uniforms?"

Ellen laughed, "Neither. I had to give that woman who wears low-cut blouses and makes good cookies a ride to the game in Alma and turns out, get this, her actual given name is Trixie and is a very nice person."

"Did she explain why she dresses slutty?" asked Mrs. M. "Honestly the only acceptable explanation would be that she is a Vice cop."

Ellen replied, "Close, cocktail waitress but she used to be an exotic dancer. So, I guess I shouldn't invite her to play Mah Jongg."

"I'm going to have to do a hard ass pass on that idea," Mrs. M. stated. "I'm glad however that you are enlarging your circle of friends, even slightly slutty ones."

Kat laughed, "I think that the slightly slutty have their own little group. Remember that foursome who played in our golf league last summer and violated the dress code every single week? They were not asked back."

"Just as well," Mrs. M. "They left a trail of divots and empty wine cooler bottles everywhere they went."

CHAPTER 37

The Great Escape

Mah Jongg was canceled for two weeks due to the death of Ellen's mother-in-law. I called on the family at the funeral home and was surprised to see Lisa there with Mrs. M. They seemed to have patched things up. I didn't realize that Ellen's mother-in-law was only seventy-two years old. Since I had known Ellen, her mother-in-law had been ill, so her death was not unexpected but nonetheless sad and shocking.

When we returned to the coffee shop to play, Mrs. M. was not present. She had left for the Mediterranean days earlier with Uncle Stan. She had met me for coffee and a conversation the week before. Her last words to me were "What will be will be, keep my seat warm. I will be back, in a box or on a boat. I have made my peace with it."

Today I arrived first and was thinking of what Mrs. M. had told me and how fleeting life can be sometimes. As soon as Ellen came to the table I stood and expressed my condolences once again, and she smiled and thanked me. Kat and Molly came in together both dressed in typical Northern Michigan fashion in jeans and flannel shirts. They both had their hair back in ponytails and big smiles.

Once we started playing Mah Jongg, I asked in

general, what was happening. Molly answered excitedly, "We just broke Bill and Dean's dad, Ed out of the assisted living place."

"How did that happen?" I asked.

Kat responded, "He doesn't want to live there anymore. We went over there with Ellen and got all of his stuff, and his car and brought him over to Bill's apartment."

"Do you know what the people at the assisted living place told us?" Ellen stated. "They told us they didn't have a form to fill out if someone leaves back to the real world, because no one ever does. They seemed confused."

Kat added, "Ed is fine on his own, he only moved in there because it was a safer environment for his wife. Bless her heart, she's gone now. Why should he stay? He has his own car, and he golfs and skis, why should he stay with the bingo and bridge crowd?"

I agreed and asked, "So is that apartment big enough for Bill and his dad?"

"Oh no," Molly replied with a wink towards me. "Bill is moving into my house."

I let out a surprised gasp, "I'm shocked but happy for you."

Molly said, "I'm happy for everyone at this point."

I had to agree.

www.ingramcontent.com/pod-product-compliance
Lightning Source LLC
Chambersburg PA
CBHW050413110726
47899CB00008B/2697